D1524168

Falling Leaves
[Yaprak Dökümü]

Reşat Nuri Güntekın

Translated from the Turkish by W. D. Halsey

Illustrated with caricatures from "kalem" and old photos

ISBN: 1491073969

ISBN-13: 978-1491073964

İstanbul Boğaz İçi Bebek

Falling Leaves

I

---Why did I resign from Goldleaf Limited? There's nothing to explain. I couldn't live on the 62 lira I made per month. I'm supporting two younger brothers and a sick mother... Mother is continually complaining about the cold, my brothers about the food. I shake my shoulders: "What can I do, it goes only so far. If I spent what I got on dancing and night clubs, you would be right to criticize; but my accounts are public knowledge!" How wonderful it would be if they grasped this obvious truth. If they didn't, I would say: "Ladies and gentlemen, if you don't like the food at this hotel, you can pay less money. If you know of a better one, let's all go there at once." and I would walk off stamping as if I had knocked on the broken door. My mother is an old woman, my brothers are two wretches of God … As soon as I proposed to rebuke them, their sails sank into the water. But with the big beast, I mean myself, what kind of reasoning would you use? I have reached the age of thirty, in a position of health and strength … my nature is spoiled – my mind wants whatever I see … I want to eat whatever I see, to wear the clothes I see … And I say I am right, even if it came to more things than

3

these… You can imagine what a tumult broke out in my heart, when my work was like this!

As, deeply wounded by the cold mud seeping into the holes of my shoes, I went home by a roundabout way to avoid the stores where I owed credit, luxury cars passed by my shoulder. I recognized some of the people in them … they were going to enjoy themselves spending money by the handful. This twisted me up inside. I said to myself, "Are they all so different from me? While they live and enjoy life to the fullest, why am I exiled to the streets like a dog? Why can't I for once embrace a woman I desire?"

After running through these arguments with myself for months and years, at last I came to this decision, "My father was a very well thought-of man … he used to say 'The most precious legacy a father leaves his children is a good name…' A good name, but it would be wonderful if it came with a little scratch. But with poor descendants, it will last only one or at most two generations. But in any event, whether my father did well or poorly is another matter… But all of these rich men around me weren't drawn from their mothers' wombs with check books under their arms… They discharged their duties and spent money instead of spending on things that God has put into men's heads, like saying "ebced[1]", things that are useless whether you are dead or alive… Since you assert it's not something stupid and senseless like a donkey, aren't the arm and hand connected? You too can cry into emptiness like a beggar, you too can try your fortune, how wonderful if you are successful… if not, you can say 'What can I do, I did what I could' but you bore the weight of blind fortune's judgement."

*

**

The man saying these words, who had resigned from the firm's

---

[1] "ebced" is a meaningless word used to remember the order of letters in the Arabic alphabet.

4

accounting department a month earlier, was a sallow faced dark-haired youth with sharp white teeth. That day he had come back to pick up some of his belongings he had forgotten and also to visit "his old comrades."

It was the noon break. The well-off clerks had gone to the dairy restaurant opposite, to eat egg salad, head cheese, bean stew. Those who didn't have money to squander on that kind of luxury and excess satisfied their bellies with cheese, olives, and hardboiled eggs while listening to their friend. He stretched out at length on one of the tables and continued his speech while striking at scattered papers with his shoe heels:

"As soon as I had definitely made up my mind to do a few things in this way, I took heed of what I saw as I looked around me. There was a bunch of bearded and mustachioed men arranged in rows like school children, we were counted in our places and added up into a strange herd... in front of my position how much striving and struggling there was, by my side how much useless pushing and shoving... I don't know how many years will pass and how many monthly paychecks will be added together. Someone will be fired, another will die, and you will get two steps ahead. For that reason I said, 'The nation gets the head, the crow the carcass," and I got out of this procession, or in other words, Goldleaf Limited... Is it a month that we have been separated? Perhaps not even that much... Didn't I immediately put my rags in order?' "

He sat up in place and laughed as he displayed with pride his imaginary silk stockings and new shirt:

"But what am I doing that is wrong? Am I meddling with anyone's property, life, honor? Not at all... I'm only working with a salesman in Haviar Hani... I pass property through customs on his account... Now the salary is small, even the kickbacks are relatively small, but with God's blessing I'll get along like a rose..."

An old man with a cough, after clearing his chest deeply, said, "You are right... what a pity it's too late for us." Two rows of sulky faced twenty-year old children were looking at him with astonishment and envy, as if he were a victorious sports champion. The only face he couldn't decipher was that of a fortyish clerk with one side burned in the war. Leaning his chin against his fist with his lunch half eaten, he was covering his eyes and thinking.

The young man got down from the table. After lighting a cigarette from the fire in the stove mouth, he began to walk around and tell tales of his profiteering and kickbacks in customs and Haviar Hani. Most of these were fables exaggerated by adding a thousand cases to one case. But these desperate men accepted as reality that while other men shoveled up gold by the shovelful, they themselves were lamenting in this damp room that they were worn out and half hungry for a few lira. Meanwhile the eyes of the story-teller grazed a dark corner of the room and the eyes of an old man looking at him from behind a high writing desk. Suddenly he felt ashamed and fell silent as if he had lost his courage.

This man, Master Ali Riza by name, was a sixty year old ex-governor. At the desk in the corner of the room, as if in the middle of a desert, forever alone and forgotten, he would work without talking with anyone.

Since he was a very good and cultured man, everyone, both young and old, respected him.

Master Ali Riza was one of the clerks who didn't go out for the noon meal. While he was eating the dry meat-balls and green olives he had brought in his aluminum lunch pail, interested in this unusual conversation, he left his fork and raised his head, as if his appetite was cut off by what he heard.

The guest blushed as if caught in an offense. But smiling, not wanting to make his embarrassment plain, he said:

"Sir, my talk has not been welcome to you, but what can I do so that really …"

Master Ali Riza answered him with the embarrassment of a schoolboy:

6

"You know that I don't meddle in people's affairs, you are free to do whatever suits your pleasure and advantage. But if you permit, I will reproach you from another quarter. Is it right to awake rebellions and certain desires that would not occur in men who work in their own corner and who perhaps are satisfied with their own conditions, their own lives? I leave it to your conscience … if you think about it, you will agree I am right."

It was clear that the old clerk did not want to say anything more, but the guest didn't leave it. He said with a cultured expression:

"Sir you would be right if I were the only one saying these bitter truths to them, but what use is it when modern men learn these truths not from one another but from the things that the newspapers *"Life"* and *"The Economist"* say about life…

Especially since the Great War a strange awakening has taken place in the whole world. Men of today are no longer men of your time… The opening of their eyes has increased their desires and ambitions. No one is satisfied any longer with his own condition. As a consequence of this movement, do you think it possible for the rules of the old ethics not to collapse and be changed?"

Master Ali Riza turned yellow, but he smiled trying not to show the light quivering of his lips and beard:

"I am an old man. It is not possible for me to understand. I have lived my life believing than man can be happy with something besides money. I will die with that belief."

The young man answered Master Ali Riza with a bitter expression:

"You are not completely wrong, for example take a man employed in religion or music. His one consolation is bringing up children, flowers, or vegetables. But for this you have to have at least a little money to live on. You worry about the flower; but if there is not the littlest bit of money? No matter how hard you try, it is obvious that you will not get the flower of the scent and color you want from dirt… There is your father, your children, and no money? At the end of your life, your descendants won't give you pleasure apart from a tragic sight of leaves falling."

His speech ended here. Master Ali Riza again bent his head to his meal. But he could no longer swallow.

Above all, the last words had badly affected him. He was the father of five children. None of these had completely left the nest. When this man said, "*Life* and *The Economist* teach these bitter realities to men" it was not an empty speech.

His whole life, he had tried to impart good thoughts and good morals to his children. Would this air of the new times shake them up too, so that they would seem to their old father in the end falling leaves?

Master Ali Riza was not a man without insight. This fear had gripped him a few times before. But the danger had never seemed so close. In spite of the fact that he was not religious, not the type to wait for something from heaven, he began to pray: "O Lord, take care of my children," as he spread his hands wide.

II

Master Ali Riza by training and education was a state employee. Until the age of thirty he had worked in one of the Interior Ministry offices.

Perhaps he would have worked there until he died. But when his sister and mother both died within the space of two months, he suddenly lost his enthusiasm for Istanbul, and this caused him to take a district governorship and go into exile in Syria.

He had imagined like most of those who have no experience of illness that the foremost means of escaping the bed where a man has suffered afflictions is to change place and get away from the things around them.

From then on, Master Ali Riza never returned to Istanbul; for twenty years he wandered from one post to another in Anatolia ...

He was a learned diligent man. But the kind of learning he was diligent at was not the type that was of practical use.

Besides Arabic and Persian, he also knew English and French. He had studied literature in his youth, he had published correctly scanned lyric poetry in reviews. And he also had a passion for philosophy and history. Not only his free time, but also his time at work was spent reading books. This was the only thing, in his long civil service career, that he stole from the state treasury.

He was clean to the point of being called fastidious; elegant to the point of being called ridiculous. To be unjust, to do anything against the law, was something that seemed totally impossible, because he would have been afraid of breaking his heart.

His desire was that whatever he did would not only conform to custom and norms of refinement and humanity but be perfect in every way...

10

They said about him, "He is a good man, a man like the prophet... kiss his hand, he discourses on learning, recites poetry, do what you do, but don't ask him to do anything!"

He was approaching forty when he got married. To set up a family in his opinion was as momentous an undertaking as setting up a nation. For this reason he might have never got married; but when one evening a close friend proposed a girl who was one of his relatives, Master Ali Riza, being ashamed to say "no" answered "certainly."

Fortunately his wife was very dignified and clean. In spite of their assurances that she was twenty, she was easily a good twenty-five. Master Ali Riza showed a faculty in the area of population growth which he never showed in any other of the state's requirements. Within seven years, one after another, he brought five children into the world. Finally, after a rest period of four years, on the day when he turned fifty, with his last girl he completed the half dozen. Of these children, five survived. The second son, Nejdet, had died from diphtheria at the age of three.

Sometimes when Master Ali Riza was still writing strophes and lyric poetry in his free time, there was a comparison that he was quite fond of: Events were like a big wave, and he himself was like a man observing the wave from a distance. Although he had become quite an important official, he would never be carried away by the wave, in his life he would always remain in an observer's position. Moreover, it was a vain labor to attempt to turn events from their pre-ordained channel. As it had come, thus it would go.

But five children coming in order one after another forced Master Ali Riza to change this attitude. Since he had to raise five children, he couldn't remain in the position of a simple observer of life. From that time, the old lax and unambitious official was gone, replaced by a pater familias who could risk every sacrifice for his children.

He never tired working day and night for his children, rather it made him happy. There was only one concern: Had he had not waited too late?

Sometimes in his tired and pessimistic moments, this reflection left him a little unquiet. But he did not dwell too much on this thought.

"My body is strong... If some accident doesn't cause my death, I could live and work a good twenty years more," he would console himself.

These twenty years were an extremely broad calculation. If it came to it, half of this period would suffice. Although his latest child, Aisha, had not arrived opportunely. But this was not such a frightening thing. If he had to, he could leave the tasks relating to her to the older children, his eye would not be needed to supervise. Granted that they were brought up as he planned...

But an event that had not occurred to his mind turned Master Ali Riza's calculations upside down, by forcing him to quit his civil service post at fifty-five.

At that time he was governor in one of the sanjaks of Trebizond. One day there was a story of a woman who ran away, and the woman's husband and the man with whom she ran away stabbed each other.

The husband was a farmer without backers, the other was the son of one of the notables whom all the townspeople obeyed. For this latter, he was forced to close his eyes and not investigate vigorously the real causes of the crime, but damage someone's reputation by throwing a man with chest wounds into prison. Henceforth Master Ali Riza made it his business not to get involved, but he lost his enthusiasm, and struggled to the extent that it caused him to resign. What could he do? This was a duty, a matter of honor and reputation. If he was lacking in doing his duty, God would hurt him in his children.

Master Ali Riza passed a certain amount of time jobless in Istanbul. He had no cash. How could a governor, the father of five children, economize? Thank God there was an old house in Bağlarbaşı, inherited from his father. He got a little ahead by selling some of his wife's jewels to eke out the children's expenses. This made him very ashamed. He could have borne death from hunger, he no longer wanted to be a civil

12

servant. But what use was it, there were the children. For their sake he was forced to be a beggar and work four or five more years.

Master Ali Riza began to haunt the corridors of the Sublime Porte[2], looking for a new governorship. One day, a tall young man coming out of the office of the Interior Ministry approached him, and took his hand and began kissing it:

"Don't you recognize me, teacher? It's your old student Muzaffer," he said.

After looking carefully, Master Ali Riza recognized him. For a period in a prep school in one of his governorships, for five or six months, he had substituted for a sick history teacher. This Muzaffer at that time was a student in the school. Since he had been a clever and industrious child, he had left Master Ali Riza with a good impression. If this young man came out

---

[2] The Sublime Porte, babiali, high gate in Ottoman Turkish, was the gate that led to the assemblage of governmental buildings in Istanbul from which the Ottoman Empire was run, hence the name of the gate came to refer to all of the Ottoman governmental offices. (Wikipedia)

from the Minister of the Interior with a bold expression, and was talking and laughing so openly in the corridor, clearly he must have gotten quite far. A little after, Master Ali Riza learned that he was not mistaken in this impression.

Muzaffer was a member of the governing council of two big companies and the general director of Goldleaf Limited. When he learned his old teacher's situation, he made a proposal. It was not right at his age for him to go into the provinces. Since the company did business with England and Egypt, they had a special need for an employee who knew Arabic and English. He knew how valuable a man his teacher was. If he wanted, the company would give him the money he made from the state, even a lot more. Master Ali Riza accepted this proposal with great joy. Even if the company gave him not more than he got from the state, but most of it, he would have pulled him to his head and kissed him.

From now on, he did not want to leave Istanbul. His children had grown. He could not drag them around with him throughout the whole country as he used to.

For five years, the ex governor was the best employee of Goldleaf Limited. He worked from morning to evening without stopping, producing the work of three men. Basically there were two reasons for this: the first was not to make Muzaffer regret the service he had done, the second he saw was from the work of translation, consisting in "being an eternal go-between" so as not to endanger the rights of anyone else from words…

III

An old attendant came to Master Ali Riza's side.

"Master, a woman has come, she wants to see you. She seems to be Mistress Leman's mother," he said.

Leman was the company typist. Master Ali Riza had become acquainted

14

with her ten or twelve years before in one of his governorships; at that time she was a sixteen year old girl, the daughter of a forest supervisor. She would sometimes come to play with his daughters.

A year ago, on the Üsküdar wharf, Master Ali Riza had crossed paths with a beautiful young girl, who had artlessly kissed his hand as she said, "I'm Leman, your daughters' friend, Uncle Master." Leman had lost her father five years before. Now she and her mother lived together in Fındıklı. They were scraping by with great difficulty. The young girl poured out her situation to Master Ali Riza without being asked. Although there had not been a very close friendship between him and her father, the fact that Leman could by age have been one of his own children was sufficient to awake in the old man a deep desire to help. Leman did not seem to have had regular schooling, but could read and write, and, what is more, had learned to type a little. Master Ali Riza did what he could, and hired her for the company at a salary of 45 lira.

This was not the end of the good that the old man wanted to do for the girl. He wanted to act as her father, to protect her from the dangers that threatened girls of this age. What today could happen to this poor girl, tomorrow could happen to his own children. But after a few weeks, he saw with regret that this in fact was coming somewhat late.

Although Leman was a very clean girl, she was flighty and injudicious. She didn't know how to control herself and would make inappropriate jokes to the company's employees.

Master Ali Riza warned her several times. The young girl heard him out and said he was right, seemingly ashamed of what she had done. But before a half hour was up, she would begin the same inappropriate jokes again.

The day came when Master Ali Riza could not hold out and had to rebuke her. The young girl at once became cross, and said she would not submit to anyone's meddling. Master Ali Riza thank God had done her a great service by placing her in the company. But his constant nagging, interfering in everything she did, was not right.

15

The old man bent forward with a bitter smile: "You are right, my child; don't be angry." But the old man from that day on neither mentioned Leman's name nor looked her in the face. Only when he saw some of her pleasantries that were almost scandalous in nature, he would get angry at himself, saying, "What did I say, I was the cause of her coming here."

For sixteen days Leman had not been seen in the firm. Probably she was ill. However he did not think to ask or search further.

Up till now, he had never seen Leman's mother face to face. What could she want from him to make her come here?

"Welcome, sister, what can I do for you?" he asked.

The woman did not answer at once. Her body and hands were trembling as if she had malaria. The old man raised his eyes in astonishment. Her face looked drawn and her eyes were swollen from crying. An evil suspicion passed through his mind. Forgetting his anger at Leman, he said: "How is Leman?"

The woman's weeping gave her answer. "Leman is well, but it would be better if she had died…"

Master Ali Riza, after he had soon learned the truth, acknowledged the old mother was right: Yes it would have been better for Leman to have died than to meet with this calamity…

This was the true story:

The director, Master Muzaffer, had seduced her.. Ten days earlier, Leman had taken leave of her mother, saying, "I'm invited to my friend's wedding on the Island." The child had ended up in a hospital! Yesterday they had brought her back home, all skin and bones… she had told everything to her mother…

Master Ali Riza seemed to have had a stroke. His hands and feet were pins and needles, he covered his face, raving with shame and fear as if he himself had corrupted the girl, beating himself and saying: "Vah, vah,

16

vah…"

The old woman looked as if she wanted to wrap herself around his feet, imploring him: "We don't have anyone but you… What will become of us? Teach us what to do… You have children…"

Master Ali Riza's emotion came not from the fact that a rake had destroyed a girl, but because he himself had been the cause of this business.

Was it not so, that if he had not hired this girl, this catastrophe wouldn't have happened? The old woman had run to him as an old family friend, because she knew no one else. But Master Ali Riza seemed to find a meaning in her words, as if she was saying, "Clean up what you did!" The old man, after he had come to himself a little, consoled the woman:

"Sister… I won't say, 'Don't worry!' I won't guess where this business will end up… But I'll do what I can… Master Muzaffer is someone I have known from childhood… His conscience won't let him see a girl be openly disgraced… He'll take Leman in marriage… He'll repair the evil he has done… Don't be sad… There's a natural goodness in men."

However this simple and uneducated woman, who had lived within four walls up to this point, was not willing to agree with this prosperous well-groomed administrator, that there was a natural goodness in men and went off as she had come, weeping.

IV

The matter had come to a head. There was no time to lose: it was necessary to meet Muzaffer Bey and clean his own reputation as well as that of these wretched people.

In Master Ali Riza's opinion, the director had injured his reputation by getting involved with a girl whom he himself had brought in and protected. A few months before, he had seen a pay increase of eighteen

17

lira. At that moment, he had heard a drunken and dissolute employee saying, "Certainly it couldn't be a protector who causes my salary to go up!"

Master Ali Riza did not attach any great importance to the speech at that time; but now he remembered it with terror, giving it an altogether different meaning. Everyone was not as unaware as he was. The others had considered the relationship between the director and Leman extremely suspicious, and they had incorrectly seen his fingers in this affair as well.

And those who still treated him with respect, who knew what they were saying behind his back!

At his age and after such a pure life, would this too fall on his head?

Meanwhile, he thought of leaving without seeing Muzaffer at all. Of his possible courses of action, this would be the most pure. But he did not persist in this opinion. He was totally involved. After this affair of the director, he could not remove all suspicion in a manner consistent with the conduct of a man of reputation.

As luck would have it, that day the work was very difficult at the firm. The director's office was like a beehive. Master Ali Riza was afraid that he would lose courage if he didn't meet Muzaffer in hot blood. He imagined his courage of the afternoon would pass into uncertainty; he decided to wait until nightfall if it was necessary.

That day the old employee didn't work until evening; in his chair he prepared what he was going to say to Muzaffer. He saw it all so vividly that he couldn't resist his emotions and began to cry, once or twice wiping his eyes with the tip of his handkerchief.

*

**

Summer or Winter, whether there was work or not, Master Ali Riza was

18

at work by nine o'clock every day.

In spite of this, he didn't leave in the evening with everyone else, he would work until nightfall.

When the director ran into him at that hour, he said, "My teacher, again you stayed late, you never have pity on yourself... If there is something to do, leave it until tomorrow."

Master Muzaffer treated him differently from all the others, because he knew he wasn't a man to be spoiled by kindness. When he rose with his habitual respect, he made him sit down by his side, gave him a cigarette.

Master Ali Riza forgot the speech he had spent hours preparing.

His head was totally empty. In spite of this, he clearly perceived the necessity of saying something, anything, and stammered a few things at random.

Master Muzaffer did not understand at first either what he said or what he wanted. Smiling, he listened to him while scribbling numbers on the edge of an envelope in front of him. But in a moment he started and his feet turned to water, while his expression and countenance began little by little to change.

The old man had hoped that he would blush, become embarrassed and confused. However he was assuming the serious expression of a man preparing to do battle, and he bewildered the wretched man by staring fixedly into his eyes.

The old employee, despite the tightness in his chest and the confusion in his head, understood in a moment that the man sitting opposite him was an altogether different man from the image he had formed over the years. The beautiful manners he had seen to this point were the product of the fact that he was only considered a harmless well educated old man.

Yes, this was a fearsome disappointment. The poor man, having called out to a far off rock, did not understand that it was something different from the echo of his soft and tentative voice. Now when he was putting his hand on it, he was learning from what kind of steel it was made!

He had no doubt the game was lost.

Muzaffer was not one of those men who make a sport of their lives and advantages, allowing others to stick their noses into his business. It took no time for Master Ali Riza to know this, but he continued to turn round and round in circles as if he had dove into a whirlpool.

The Director, after waiting a little more, interrupted him at a random point. "I understand; with your permission let me also speak a little. You cannot doubt the respect and love I feel for you. You are too good, a different kind of man from those of today, of this world. I won't tell a lie. Leman's story is true. Would that it had not happened! I too want that. But what can I do, it happened. But believe me that this story isn't such a big deal as you make it out. According to my understanding, you propose that I marry this girl. Let's speak openly. This is impossible. If you want to go further, this wouldn't be the right thing. Because I am not the first to seduce Mistress Leman.

This speech struck Master Ali Riza like a whip. The old man straightened up. "My master, my boy … It is a sin … Whatever you say, Leman was a girl, so high, like my finger.." he tried to say a few things.

But Muzaffer interrupted him again. Smiling at the old man's naivety, he said. "Master, believe me, I won't lie to you. Leman is not as innocent as you think… She would lie down and rise with whoever was in front of her. And if you want I can prove it. There was even doubt that I was the father of the child. However, perhaps reasonably, the girl thought I was a more suitable father than the others. Ah, Master Ali Riza … I wish the world were as you think!"

In spite of the director's insistence, Master Ali Riza, trembling violently, got to his feet. "So there isn't anything you can do for this poor child? I ask this question because I doubt that my conscience is entirely clean."

"I can only help by giving her money… As a matter of fact, I had her speak with me about this."

"This is all you can do?"

"Nowadays do you think there can be a greater commitment for a man than to help with money?"

The young man said this with a slight admixture of pity and ridicule. But, changing his expression again, he added with a gentle seriousness. "You are my teacher; in this regard you are almost my father. And I am going to ask you a question. Do you think it proper for me to marry a woman who is in this position? A little while ago, I was speaking to you because, just like you when you spoke to me, I too did not doubt my humanity and my conscience. You are a father. If your son had done what I did, would you make this recommendation to him too?"

Master Ali Riza was badly agitated. He thought for a moment with his eyes closed. If it had really been his own son who had done this, would he take a compromised woman like Leman in his home, stick her among his own pure children, call her "daughter-in-law"?

The old man would lose his case by answering "no". But in spite of this, he preferred to lose this hopeless case rather than telling a lie; with a desperate expression, he said, "You are right, I would not accept her."

The director, happy to have got hold of him in a delicate place, and wanting to tie him up tighter, said, "Then, what do you think, especially since I'm your student, in effect your heir?"

Absolutely expecting the answer that he wanted, he was staring into the old man's eyes.

But Master Ali Riza bent his head down with a angry obstinacy. "If my son did such a thing, what I would do is obvious: I would renounce him, I would never see him again face to face."

"Master Ali Riza, let's calm down. This girl is clearly trying a stratagem, she wants to marry me. This is not possible; but instead I will help her as much as I can. I will increase her salary, in addition I'll pay damages. She and her mother will escape penury."

The director came beside Master Ali Riza.

With the gentlest of touches he massaged his shoulders, tried to raise his spirits.

"How wonderfully generous you are! Too generous... My poor fellow, you're worn out by worry..."

The old man raised his eyes from the floor and smiled with great sadness.

"I'm worn out by worry.. It's true, I'm totally worn out.. But I'm worn out not as you suppose by worry about that girl, but about my own children."

"How does this have to do with your own children?"

"Because I must leave you over this affair. Perhaps the children will go hungry..."

Master Muzaffer perceived at once that this was not a pleasantry, an empty threat. But he pretended that he didn't understand, didn't believe him. "What are you saying? What have I done to you? Have I wronged you?"

Master Ali Riza, with the calm the comes from taking a irrevocable decision, and with great logic in comparison to his previous confusion, began to speak. "On the contrary, you have helped me greatly. You took me by the hand at a most difficult time. You have always treated me with delicacy and respect. I am indebted to you for this. But how can I remain here after this affair? Remember the words that I just spoke. Didn't I say, 'If my son did something like this, I would renounce him, we would no longer see one another' And you are another son. Therefore I am forced to renounce you. You have put your hand on a girl who came here through me. I am like your procurer... Even if it wasn't really like that, how could you explain it to everyone? The bread that I and my family,

22

like Leman's mother, would eat from this house couldn't possibly be clean."

Now Master Muzaffer was flustered in earnest by the seriousness of this business.

He tried to cut him off, saying "My teacher, I beseech you, let me speak too!" But Master Ali Riza shook his head stubbornly and continued:

"There's no need, I know what you're going to say. Perhaps you are even correct… But these are not things that my old head can accept…"

The director understood that he wouldn't be able to break the old employee's obstinacy.

"My teacher, at least ask me if I can be of some other help."

Master Ali Riza smiled with the simplicity of a child:

"From now on I can accept nothing from you. You are worried about what I will do? As long as I'm not altogether dead, we will certainly find a way."

"And we won't see each other again?"

"Certainly my child, there is no way."

When Master Ali Riza spoke these words, he knew with total certainly that they would never come face to face, not even in the last judgement.

V

That evening Master Ali Riza did not find an omnibus cab because he had waited until the last steamboat. It was not the first time this had happened to him.

When he passed the evening in the company, he would take a hackney cab costing about forty or fifty piastres. What could he do, this was a professional necessity.

That evening as well, when he left the wharf, he made his way deep in thought to the place where the cabs waited. But, all of a sudden, he remembered that he was unemployed, unsalaried.

From now on, he had no right to luxuries. He turned around. Four or five peddlers were crying at him at the top of their lungs to come and buy at once the last fruits and vegetables they had in their baskets.

Master Ali Riza hesitated for a moment in front of them. Their wares were at their worst and most spoiled but the prices had fallen to half of what they were in the morning. Besides this, he preferred not to shop at such an hour. But why hadn't he considered such slight advantages in price earlier?

He made his way slowly and heavily through the lonely Üsküdar streets. He began to clamber up the ascent of the Karajaahmet Cemetery. Master Ali Riza paid as little attention to the road as he could. Still, when he saw

24

the hill in front of him, his chest was constricted.

While he was in this state, in the evening when he should have been at his most dead tired, he felt a strange power in his body. Sometimes he thought of sitting down on one of the stones at the side of the road. But he didn't have the courage. This fear wasn't the result of the loneliness of the road or the graves beside it.

On the contrary, in spite of the fact that ordinarily he was a rather fearful man, this evening he had been seized by a great fearlessness and indifference to every sort of danger. But if he began to sit and reflect, he thought that an unexpected hopelessness would come from the depth of the night around him among the cypresses and he would collapse and never escape from the claws of this despair.

That night, Master Ali Riza's house seemed unusually brightly lit. At first he thought it was a vague fancy caused by his long walk in the darkness.

But when he approached more closely, he saw that he had seen correctly. This evening there something going on in the house that was inexplicable and different. The garden gate was open. Inside, torches were burning around the trees. When he was still rather far away, he had heard the cry of Aisha's treble saying, "He's coming!" What was stranger, his daughters, and his wife, who never even came out into the garden unless there was some very important affair, ran to the street to greet him. Whatever could be the reason for this? This evening didn't it seem necessary for him to be greeted in greater silence and darkness than usual?

In spite of his extraordinary bewilderment, Master Ali Riza didn't ask them anything, nor did they say anything.

Aisha seized her father's hand with emotion and swiftly led him inside.

At last, at the head of a decorated table set up under the garden bower, they gave him the news.

His oldest son Shevket had won a contest, and had become the employee of a bank at a monthly salary of 100 lira.

For the second time that day, Master Ali Riza turned his eyes to the firmament. O God, what luck! 100 lira ... At once almost the same monthly sum that he had lost. It was like in a war when a wounded soldier sees another rise from the place where he has fallen, taking the weight from his shoulders and the weapon from his hands to continue the fight.

Master Ali Riza had educated his son from earliest infancy, saying, "After me, you are the head of this family, if I die you will take over my place!"

The old man, pressing his son's light, chestnut-haired head to his chest, was totally incapable of hiding the tears in his eyes.

The children until that day had not seen their father weeping. But they thought that all these tears came from love and pride.

VI

Master Ali Riza's son Shevket was his oldest child. Two months ago he had had his twentieth birthday. He was rather well-educated. He knew the language especially well. However this was all due to the efforts of his father, rather than to his schools, because, as befitted the children of an itinerant employee, he had not stayed in any school more than two or three years.

Master Ali Riza had played with this first child as an amateur gardener plays in the garden, and had formed him solely to be the model of a perfect man, living as an image of himself. Shevket had learned a great many things, although most were not things the world has created for today, or even for any day. In Master Ali Riza's mind, because his son was a perfect man, thus a lofty education was necessary. Who cared if he had not asked his permission? But in spite of this, Shevket could not be called half-formed.

Because at this age he was not running with youths who had studied in the High Schools of Istanbul and Europe, he was formed to come to the aid of his aged father, at his hour of greatest need. The latest success, like help coming from Heaven, was the most shining evidence of this.

But Master Ali Riza's most profound impression on Shevket, was not in his head, but in his heart. The old employee suspected everything in the world, but not his son's morals. In his opinion, Shevket was a diamond that no power in the world could break or sully.

This trust in his child was the real reason he had kicked "Goldleaf Limited" away so cavalierly. However, he didn't expect the help he was counting on would come so quickly.

Shevket was as proud as his father. Perhaps because he thought he might not win, and be diminished, he had hidden from his family the fact that he had entered the contest.

As regards the light in the house and the table in the garden, this was one of Shevket's very oldest promises. Master Ali Riza, on the day when he had started Shevket in his first school, had said: "I want a turkey dinner from you on the day when you grow up and become an employee."

In spite of the long years that had passed in the meantime, he hadn't forgotten his promise, and that morning when he saw his name in the newspaper at the head of the winners of the contest, the first thing he did was run to the market and buy two turkeys.

Everyone in the household, big or little, participated in preparing this party. Mistress Hayriye and the oldest daughter Fikret worked in the kitchen, Laila and Nejla prepared the table, and Aisha brought bunches and bunches of flowers she had gathered from the neighboring gardens.

Master Ali Riza had completely forgotten the disaster that had happened a little earlier. Only when it was time to sit in the chair prepared for him at the head of the table, he paused and thought. Then smiling meaningfully at his son, he said, "Let's change places, Shevket. You'll be the father, I'll be the oldest child."

Everyone was bewildered.

But he insisted, he commanded, and pulling his son's sleeve he said, "I want it this way, you must obey me."

Master Ali Riza, with the expression of a king who is forced to abdicate in favor of his son, made Shevket sit in his place. He sat at his left, beside his wife.

"Sooner or later this will be his place in the family. Do you hear, children? The time has come when you will recognize and count him as your father instead of me."

The old man did not betray the disaster that had happened to him by anything other than the weighty inflexion his voice took on as he said these words.

There was no reason to alarm his family any more on this night. Especially since, before Shevket got the news of the heavy responsibility to be placed on his shoulders, this was the last night he could sleep in peace and happiness.

VII

Master Ali Riza, was used to getting up early with his adult son and his wife. They were forced to do this because the three of them had very different duties inside and outside the home.

But the world had not yet turned difficult for the girls. There was no problem now if they spent a few lazy hours in bed. In spite of the fact that from now on he would be included among the house's lazybones, that morning he rose even before the dawn. As he did every day he picked up a book and sat in front of the window. But he was completely incapable of reading. While his wife lit the fire and prepared the morning

28

tea, he was plunged in thought in front of an open page.

After breakfast, Mistress Hayriye began to prepare her husband's lunch. Master Ali Riza said, blushing: "It isn't necessary, Mistress... Don't take the trouble..."

Knowing that, even on stormy days when the steamboat wasn't running, he never missed even one day of work, Mistress Hayriye was alarmed. "Are you sick?" she asked.

"No, I'm not going."

When Master Ali Riza said this, he looked like a troublesome child who didn't want to go to school because he was angry at the teacher.

"Why?"

The old man caressed Shevket, who had just sat down beside him, on the face. Trying to hide his emotion, he said: "I have something to discuss with Shevket. After my son has listened carefully to me, he will give his judgement... Whatever he says, I am prepared to accept."

Master Ali Riza was speaking in such a tone, and with such an expression, that his wife and his son were looking at one another and could not make out whether if this was really a joke or not.

The old man explained what had happened. Because he was not accustomed to speak openly and frankly with his son, when he came to the shameful parts of the story, he would glance to the side and his voice became indistinct. On Mistress Hayriye's face, nothing but bewilderment could be read. But while Shevket was listening to his father, little by little he was suffused with emotion, and his black eyes began to sparkle with a strange fire. When his father had finished the recital and asked, "In the face of the circumstances, could I have done anything but resign?" he said, without the slightest hesitation:

"You did well, papa!"

The was such a spirit of rebellion in this phrase that Master Ali Riza with difficulty restrained himself from wrapping his arms around his son and openly weeping.

With an embarrassed expression, he bent his neck down and asked the essential question: "My son, there is only one thing that we must also discuss... This company was my last source of bread... You know me... I don't want to sit and twiddle my thumbs... But perhaps I won't find work from now on... You know your sisters must still be brought up... My pension is very small.. The whole burden of the family will fall on your shoulders... Won't this seem hard for you?"

Shevket was almost offended by his father's doubt. He struck his chest with the boundless courage of twenty years old: "How dare you say this to me, papa? Do you doubt me? If it's necessary, I will do anything and more. However it is to be managed, we will bring up my sisters!"

Shevket now understood why his father had sat him in his place at the table yesterday. Though he was embarrassed by these circumstances, he was almost proud to become head of the family at his age. The father and son kissed one another with emotion.

*

**

A little later, when Master Ali Riza was alone with his wife, he laughed with pleasure: "What happiness for a father!"

Mistress Hayriye, occupied with her meticulous cleaning of the table, said, without turning her head: "Yes… You are right…"

The woman's countenance was somehow sulky, and the words barely issued from her mouth. Master Ali Riza was nervous: "Why are you answering with half your mouth?" he asked.

Mistress Hayriye said, a little crossly, "What difference does it make, half or all? I said, 'You are right.'"

"No, you were really saying something different."

The woman left her work and turned to look at Master Ali Riza.

"Don't be cross, but you have become silly with age."

"Frankly, that's what you are!"

When he said this, he expected a protest from his wife, but she turned back to her work without answering. The matter was growing more serious, and a fear whose cause was unknown began to compress Master Ali Riza's chest.

Master Ali Riza felt a strange trepidation whenever he bought something unnecessary for the house or spent money on someone out of softness or pity; his wife, however, wasn't at all the type to comfort him, saying, "There's no harm done... Don't be worried, what can we do... It's done..."

Rather, Mistress Hayriye was careful about accounts and property, and didn't joke about things that had to do with the welfare of the family. She didn't give the consolation her husband expected when he was worn out from worry and regret at what he had done. It was even from this very fact that the quarrel broke out between them. Master Ali Riza, because his wife was the only person he dared to quarrel with openly, became peevish like a child: "You are this way, in fact... You can't penetrate into a man's heart. By God, if I die you'll be rid of me!" he was shouting.

Mistress Hayriye, after letting him cry and wear himself out for a while and spoiling his pleasure in what he had done, changed her stratagem.

Today the old man wasn't reading things in his wife. Basically he didn't believe himself that what he had done was the right thing.

But a few sweet words from his wife would have calmed him to a degree. However, the contrary woman, not understanding that Master Ali Riza had just had the most tense and difficult day of his life, continued to knit her brows in a frown.

"Woman," he said, "Look at me! Today you're doing something that will never be forgotten if I die... Shame on you."

For the second time, Mistress Hayriye turned around, and said with a

32

sadness and sincerity that made more impression than the most savage imprecations:

"Why are you talking this way, Master Ali Riza? Someone listening to you would think you took some new rank and are pleased... We essentially barely squeaked by on the 115 lira you made from the company... Today you told me that even this is gone... This for me is honesty... Should I love you and wrap myself around your neck? You too show a little fairness!..."

Master Ali Riza, unable to find any speeches, gulped ridiculously a few times: "Yes but our name... We haven't lost our name!..."

The word "name" never failed to make a big impression on this virtuous, simple housewife. But now when hunger had knocked on their door it seemed to have lost its power. "Be fair, Master Ali Riza... I am a woman of a certain age. If you are putting me in the same category as an immoral woman it is both shameful and a sin... And I am as conscious of 'name' as you. But if I were in your place, I would shut my eyes for the sake of the children."

Master Ali Riza burst into flames at these words: "What was that you said, then? What? ... Go on... You'd close your eyes to something like that? Shame... shame on you!" he began to scream.

Mistress Hayriye raised her eyes to the ceiling. "Calm down!... you'll wake the children..."

Then she repeated with calm sadness: "Yes, Master Ali Riza! Whatever you may say... I would endure anything for their sake. Because if we have no money, their reputation is endangered..."

This observation came down on Master Ali Riza's head like a cudgel. He remembered the phrase he had heard the day before at the company from someone else. "Reputation without money lasts one or two generations." These two almost identical opinions had come from the mouths of two people who were worlds apart from one another. What fearsome power it was that had impelled two different people who didn't know one another to speak in the same way!

While Master Ali Riza sought the answer to this riddle in his confused brain, the woman continued to speak bitterly: "Don't be angry, Master Ali Riza... I'm going to say what is in my heart... You are always sacrificing the interests of the children to vague fears. You think because they have reached the age of 15 or 20 that your job is over. It's not! Your real job is now beginning... They used to be little bitty dolls. They sat where you said, 'Sit!', they ate when you said 'Eat!' If you put a penny whistle and a broken doll in their hands, they partied as if you had given them the world. Each one of these children has now become a big person. They understand everything, they want everything... What are the desires of each one of them? I don't know but most probably educating them was also a mistake."

"You have gone mad, Mistress... My children are such angels that..."

"I am not denying it... The children we have now seem angelic... But we have opened their minds from one side... As I said, they see everything, they want... Will they remain angelic in the future? And even if so, won't they be affected emotionally? Until now, you have worked outside the home. You haven't seen the home from inside, your children from close by... Therefore let me bring you the news, Master... Our children are in danger... The sin has come from me."

Master Ali Riza came to understand that this quarrel was not something that could be solved by a loud argument. Now he began to beg: "My dear wife... Don't be a child... I had not thought of these points... But you heard my son. He is ready to make every sacrifice for his little sisters. You don't doubt him, do you?"

"If you want the truth, I do doubt him, Master Ali Riza... However it may be, he also is a young child... He too will have desires... And even if that weren't so, isn't it a sin to place a burden on the finger thin neck of a child?"

The husband and wife would not have understood one another on this

34

point if they had argued for a year. Master Ali Riza was without doubt the best of fathers. He would not have been happy if through him the smallest injury had happened to any of his children. But he was convinced that, in making one of his children head of the family, he had given him the biggest happiness in the world. In his eyes, being head of the family was like being the Sultan.

Therefore, the idea that Shevket would complain about the burden of the family was as inexplicable as if someone who was a king found the crown that he put on his head heavy.

But Mistress Hayriye, who couldn't imagine putting this burden on a naïve head that didn't possess their wisdom, was boiling over with a wrath that increased from moment to moment.

"I believed in you like a child as surely as my hair turning grey… Why not, 'He is a bearded, mustachioed man who reads and writes, he must know something,' I said. From now on, it's over… Since 'name' compelled you to leave this job… Leave it… But don't forget that expenses increase from day to day… Look, from now on I'm not going to hide it. Your angelic children have fallen into an impossible condition. If your children begin to fall one by one in the face of destitution, my two hands, my ten fingers will be on your collar. Even if you go and die, I won't leave you in peace in your grave."

So that the children wouldn't hear any longer, the woman went into the kitchen weeping and wailing in a high voice. Master Ali Riza remained frozen in his place.

So that the woman with the head that was as soft as a yearling lamb finally raised the flag of rebellion.

A pail in his hand, he was walking in the garden, picking off the flower hips, watering the vegetables, cleaning the bugs off the saplings. But he was only thinking of his children. Doubtless his wife was an ignorant woman. But her anxiety was not totally unreasonable. The opinions she had given were not things to be idly cast off. Were his children really in

35

danger? What was worse, had there been a mistake in their education, as his wife had said? First of all, he considered his oldest daughter Fikret.

She was a small short girl of 19. But she was more serious than a thirty-year-old.

In the house, she was the most valuable helper for her mother and a second mother to her sisters despite the unimportant age difference between them. Fikret was not beautiful. What is more, there was a spot in her left eye. This spot was a souvenir of a long eye disease she had had in one of the provinces of Inner Anatolia. Perhaps Master Ali Riza would have found a cure if he been able to send the child to Istanbul at that time. What a shame that this illness had happened to occur in a period when work was at its most difficult and complicated.

But there was a peerless moral beauty in Fikret that masked all her defects.

Even the spot for Master Ali Riza was a defect of no consequence. On the contrary, it even created a different beauty by the tenderness it gave to her heart and the modesty it brought to her countenance. However not everybody, and especially not the young men who wanted to get married, saw her with the eyes of her father.

Master Ali Riza had tried to educate Fikret with the same care he gave to his son. Only, since she was a girl, and would not be thrown into life like her brother, she would not need practical knowledge. For this reason, Master Ali Riza taught her many more things of fancy and elegance.

The young girl read so many books that she endangered her sick eye, and most of these were novels.

When Master Ali Riza saw his daughter spout serious observations about life, culled from works of art and literature, he grinned from ear to ear with pleasure.

The girl had tried to be so clever and learned that it would excuse all the defects of her face. Thankfully it could not be said that she was

36

unsuccessful in this desire. Moreover, her mother educated her so that she would also be an excellent housewife. Today the child had no fault. She was capable of making any man of discernment happy. But…

In Master Ali Riza's mind, sad doubts began to be awakened.

Yes not a single one of the girl's defects was very consequential. But how would a man think about it, how would he feel about it? When their poverty increased day by day, wouldn't this become twice as difficult?

Every day a certain number of young men would come around. Most of them were either afraid of proposing marriage as if their mouths were stapled shut or else discussed it jokingly. A few also said openly that they considered it a type of trade, that is to say they were looking for a girl with money. Yes his wife was not altogether wrong. Fikret had probably been educated erroneously. Why put a wakeful spirit inside ugliness? Don't you notice more quickly where there has been neglect in something, when it is in an unbecoming place? They are useless like beautiful words in an ugly mouth, righteous words in a harsh mouth.

As Master Ali Riza Bey pondered this point, the doubts in his heart became more powerful. Yes Fikret had been educated erroneously. If this ugly girl had understanding to the extent that she desired, then in the end she would suffer to that extent. What a pity that he had not raised a girl without thought and emotions who would struggle and fight tooth and nail like a man.

But his child of today was not "peerless Fikret", and today he was disappointed in the happiness he felt when he would think of her and say "my child". But what was wrong with him? Oh well, this must be contentment!

After Fikret, Master Ali Riza thought of Leila and Nejla. They weren't as clever as their big sister. But they were beautiful in the full significance of the word. Leila was 18 and Nejla had just turned 16. At this time, finding lawful husbands of intelligence for them too was a matter of discussion. But this was not so difficult.

The young men of today couldn't see in Fikret's spirit any spark of beauty, but Leila and Nejla, thanks to their faces, could sell themselves however they wanted. The business to that day had been honorable, but as soon as he saw weaklings and wastrels, like all young man, round about, he would have to protect them from hazards.

When it came to Aisha, from of old Master Ali Riza was accustomed to think of her as the property of her siblings. Whether it was he himself or Shevket, they would always be able to protect her.

These were the children the old father thought about continuously while he worked in the garden that day.

VIII

The first days of retirement and leisure...

Like every working man he knew sooner or later the day would come when he would be thrown on the trash heap. But he had thought of that time totally differently.

When he was retired, all of his child-rearing duties would be finished and all of them would have their own households.

When he closed his eyes and thought of the future, this was the dream he always saw. The young fathers and ignorant mothers, giving themselves airs that now and again grandchildren would be born and begin to grow up, had placed the whole burden of these children on him and his wife. When he said, "It's up to you, from now on I'm retired from life, my work is nothing else but waiting for my death in a corner," they would say, "Come on, let's go!"

From now on there was no time for a grandfather to scratch his head. Sometimes he would take the kids to play in the country; at other times he would tell them fairytales by the hearth. As time passed, he would teach the adolescents his family history; then, as he had done to their

38

fathers and mothers, it would be necessary to give them lessons in morality and righteous conduct.

The result was that these times were so full of tumult and work that when the hour came he couldn't even find the time to lie on his death bed, perhaps, amongst the sounds of the children's whistles, their trumpets and drums, he would die without being noticed. For a man, could one think of a greater happiness?

This dream had now become a dream in another sense.

For a long time, one of Master Ali Riza's complaints had been that he couldn't find time to read books. Work always popped up at the sweetest part of the page he was reading. Especially in the mornings, his wife standing next to him, ramrod straight like Azrael,[3] saying, "Come on, Master Ali Riza, it's time, you'll miss your steamboat," was so annoying that…

When Master Ali Riza closed his book, he would always say, "If only I were retired!" The day that he desired had come. From now on, his wife saying "Come on, Master Ali Riza… Leave your book!" and leaving him no peace, would not happen. But, perversely, his old pleasure in books was gone.

*

**

His wife's peevishness and sourness of the first days had not passed at all. For a long time in the beginning, Master Ali Riza had remained cross with her, but when he saw she paid him no mind, he grew reconciled of his own accord.

Nothing grated on him as much as this behavior of Mistress Hayriye. One day he said to her: "Shame on you, Mistress… It's clear that you

---

[3] Azrael, the angel of death, the grim reaper.

cared for me only because of my job, the money I earned."

When he saw her lips all twisted up, that she didn't even think it was necessary to get angry, he took on a pleading expression.

"In life we were like two army buddies. Is it right to strike me in the back when they took my arms out of my hand?"

This was a speech he had been preparing for a long time. He thought that when his wife heard it she would weep and throw her arms around him, and that the conflict between them would be finished. But this speech that was very touching in Master Ali Riza's mind only made his own eyes water. Mistress Hayriye on the other hand looked at him expressionlessly, and shook her shoulders with a closed countenance:

"What can we do ... He who causes himself to fall shouldn't cry."

IX

One month had been enough to make Master Ali Riza like every other retired employee.

Like a wheel whose age is not obvious while it's still rotating, his age too, not noticed while he was working, became apparent when he suddenly stopped, along with all its ravages. The weight of his arms waving in the spaces on both sides of him began to collapse his shoulders and make him a hunchback.

His appearance and his dress became disheveled. The knee patches of his pants and the elbows of his sleeves hung loosely. Whereas in the old days how beautifully and cleanly he had dressed! The dust on him was swept off no longer, it began to work its way into his clothes.

In the morning, he would still rise together with the sun. But he no longer felt the old freshness of those hours; on the contrary, contemplating the length of the paths the sun would traverse that day, he would feel a deep emptiness in his body. The old taste was gone from his books and his garden. Like a man surprised by his deafness, who says, "Spring has come, the birds are still as always opening and shutting their mouths, but why isn't any sound coming out?", he too would think, "What happened to me is known, but what happened to the books and the flowers?"

41

Nevertheless, because of the power of habit, he still would look at his books of poetry, he would take great pains to pull up the weeds covering the garden and water the flowers. But, under the impression that a long period of time had passed, when he raised his head and saw the sun still in the same place, he was bewildered at what he would do. Morning and evening at the hour of the steamship, he was accustomed to go to the street door. His hand behind his back, walking up and down slowly and heavily along the length of the garden wall, he would look at the processions of employees going to their work and coming back with the sadness of a stork with a broken wing looking at flocks of storks in flight.

For a long time, Master Ali Riza had been the principal foe of cafés and brasseries. When he was employed, he had always said: "Who needs these dens of idlers? If it was up to me, I'd close all of them!"

Now he was starting to understand their job and how comforting their corners were for wretched retirees who had no peace or food at home.

At first, he had begun by pausing in rural cafés during the long walks that he took all the way to Çamlıca or the Üsküdar market district. Afterwards little by little he took to frequenting market or neighborhood cafés. In those first experiences, he would withdraw into a corner and read the newspaper. He had not yet got over his loathing for the habitual customers of these establishments.

They reproached him with never mingling among them. That he would never be anything but an observer among them. What he saw and heard! There were men who were so old that they related the conditions of their homes without being embarrassed, they made fun of their wives, they even sometimes talked about what they had eaten, or that they had gone hungry when they couldn't find anything to eat.

Some played continually at backgammon or cards,[4] and if someone stopped occasionally they would attack one another with unspeakable

---

[4] Literally, iskambul, from Italian, a specific card game.

curses, and afterward they would continue playing as if nothing had happened. He once even saw a retiree caught cheating get beaten up.

In Master Ali Riza's opinion, after such behavior the man should never have come back inside the café, even should have died. But on the next day, he saw him in the same café playing backgammon as if nothing had happened.

At first, he heard of one or two wretches seeking him out to have a conversation with him. Then little by little his friends multiplied. But his pride still continued.

Although he was always hearing the troubles of others, he never said one word about his own.

At last he understood that these cafés were the only temples of refuge from the afflictions born of lack of work and lack of peace in the family. And if they didn't exist, the pensioners would have nothing left to do but to die.

X

In the end, Master Ali Riza had a café and a group of nine or ten aged pensioners. What could he do, he couldn't stay still in the face of events!

Nearly all of these were old men who had difficulty getting by. They managed by continuously struggling like ants, but the results somehow didn't resemble ants so much as cicadas. Their monthly pensions in the face of their daily necessities were like the ear on a camel.

Most of these were virtuous reputable men. But some lamented, "Why didn't we work when opportunity was at hand," while others would say, "We worked, but since this was the result, why didn't we spend our time more pleasantly? Day and night we struggled and strove, after squeezing out our juice like a lemon, they threw away our pulp."

Master Ali Riza was as sorry for these men as he was for himself. But he didn't agree with them, there were even minor arguments on this subject.

Although he wasn't expecting this to have any resolution, nevertheless it was a way to pass the time.

From his new friends, Master Ali Riza learned some useful ways to buy cheaply.

How and from where could he buy coal, tallow, vegetables? Only he wasn't capable of applying any of the methods he learned, because it seemed necessary to be too familiar with tradespeople, either too obstinate or too toadying. Neither of these would ever suit Master Ali Riza's serious nature. One day when he spent a long time among the "town mayors" he went to the market with a friend. They were going to buy vegetables. A quarrel broke out with the tradesman. The shopkeeper grabbed the squashes the old town mayor was holding and said: "Go about your business, old man... You didn't come to buy but to beg... If you don't have money, gather grass from the meadow and eat that!" Then as he pushed the poor man away, he wrapped up the vegetables in his baskets. Master Ali Riza sank into the center of the earth from shame and resolved never again to go to the market with anyone.

Master Ali Riza noticed that most of his retired friends complained about their home lives. So he was not alone in this regard. Quarreling oppressed and tyrannized these poor pensioners' homes like a disease. Henceforth, Master Ali Riza believed that this inability to get by was all caused by the same cause, the damned power of "economic conditions."

In the morning the wretched old men would barely escape from their homes as if from a fire, and would sit quarrelling and dozing until midnight. However, now more than ever they needed a warm family hearth. It was because they had dreamed of these days of old age, that until now they had endured a thousand types of family trouble without a single complaint. What had they hoped, and what was the reality! God protect us if these cafés had not existed! And in these cafés, what did Master Ali Riza see and hear! The strangest thing was that whatever these old men had most feared up until now, that was the very thing that had befallen them. For example, an old secretary who had been so frightened his whole life of going into debt, that no type of moneylender's monthly bill ever escaped his hand, he was preparing to go to jail for debts to the butcher and grocer. Two times he had almost died when creditor tradesmen began to scream and yell in front of his door. But now he didn't care, he even looked at the danger of prison with philosophical resignation. "What can I do … let the rascals have their judgement. I didn't die when I took on debts; that means I won't die sleeping in prison. Prison is welcome, and no punishment that I would really fear!"

There was even an old property manager who had a great reputation for cleanliness in his youth. He would never wash and wear a stocking that he had once taken off. Now the lice paraded around this wretch's collar. Two years before, his wife had been paralyzed. There was no one else but him in the house. He took all the tasks for her on himself. Moreover day and night he put up with the invalid.

A third was beaten every evening by his daughter and her husband, he would enter the café carrying a bundle and say, "God damn me if I ever return to that house!"

But, when sleep overtook him near to the time that the regulars dispersed, when the evening frost began to pain his rheumatic feet, he changed his decision, and with his bundle again in his arm, he returned home, slowly and pensively. But rather than pitying him, they laughed, "He's going to get what he has earned!" This was right to a degree. This man, for long years in the old days a teacher in military high schools, had caned so many children!

Among the café's regulars there was one named Master Sermet, an ex governor. But he was not like the other pensioners. On the contrary, by his dress and speech it was understood that he had been a well-off man.

Master Sermet was a man with a reputation for uprightness and honor in his work life. In spite of his seventy years, he spoke with a loud voice and carried himself ramrod straight, with a ruddy face and crew cut white hair.

Like everyone, Master Ali Riza at first attached importance to the man and heard his words with respect. But afterwards, he heard bad things about Master Sermet, there was something about this man with the distinguished clothes that was much more loathsome than being beaten or lousy. According to what they said, this man's daughters were not of sound morals. Even while he was loudly discoursing in the café about morals and virtue, there were vilenesses in his home to make the hair stand on end. As a matter of fact, the cause of his being able to dress so well was that very thing.

Some said that Master Sermet wasn't aware of anything, but according to others, even if this man was such an idiot that he wasn't cognizant of the scandals befalling his family, he wasn't such a dotard as not to guess the source of the money flowing like a gutter in his home. Like a swine, he knew everything.

Although Master Ali Riza was extraordinarily hesitant to get mixed up in this gossip, one day he said with great trepidation: "This second conjecture seems improbable... How could a man bear to know such things?"

They all roared with laughter. How could one of God's creatures not bear what God gives?

At first, the wretched man, no doubt, was a little troubled. But afterwards, little by little, he grew used to it.

In short, the events in this café made Master Ali Riza forget his own troubles for a while.

XI

What a good school poverty was for Master Ali Riza! He began to see everything under its true colors, its true appearance. From now on, no one made the slightest effort to present himself to this old man without money as anything other than what he was. This extended even to his children...

In Fikret he perceived a strange distance and coldness to himself. This child too was experiencing something inexplicable in the deepest recesses of her heart. She no longer treated him as a friend and showed openly that she didn't believe in him as she used to. And in these difficult times, what were the hopes Master Ali Riza placed in this delicate and serious child!

As for Leila and Nejla, they too were in exactly the same state. Outwardly, there were no improprieties toward their father, but they would refuse to meet his gaze, as if they bore him a grudge from some unknown cause, and they would turn their heads away with a stubborn expression as if they had already decided not to believe any more in whatever they heard when he opened his mouth.

When Master Ali Riza had embarked on this adventure, he had had the highest belief in his influence and powers of persuasion over his children. This was such a tidal wave because before everyone in the house had believed in him and their obedience made it possible to embark, now however they had scattered at the first shock and were leaving him totally alone to face the great calamity.

At first the old man had blamed this defeat on Mistress Hayriye and bore a grudge against his wife, saying, "As if what she herself did wasn't enough, she has also been poisoning the children's minds and egging them on against me!" But he understood afterwards that suspecting the poor woman of this sin was groundless. Rather than her inciting the children, it was the children who were making her so bitter and cross. There was also something else that strengthened this thought. Mistress Hayriye, although distant toward her husband, had never neglected her duties as housewife.

As a matter of fact, for a long time she had been known for being extremely thrifty. Now she had taken this almost to the level of a miser, a gypsy. A man could expect nothing greater from his wife at such a low period.

*

**

As for his son Shevket, he was the only thing left that could bring happiness and consolation to his old father. What a wonderful jewel this Shevket had turned out to be! In the eyes of his father, the young man was beginning little by little to reach the level of a divinity.

He alone understood the fire that was burning Master Ali Riza. As one who had taken upon himself the whole burden of the family, irritated and worn out to the point of earning the right to make the bitterest reproaches, he didn't betray his education but when the time was right he would sit on his father's knees caressing his beard and consoling him: "Don't be afraid, daddy... I will never disappoint you... You'll see how

48

well it will turn out, how comfortable we'll be in the end... My highest priority will be to educate my sisters. Besides that, what happens to us is nothing. If you and mother are happy, I'll be happy."

Shevket was thinking completely differently from his sisters; there was only one person in the house who neglected himself...

One day Master Ali Riza sought to talk to him: "Don't lie to me, Shevket, you certainly also wanted to be something... What would you have done if this misfortune hadn't happened to us?"

Shevket thought deeply: "I wanted to be a good architect, father... To grow up, to earn money, to be famous... But what can we do... Fate can't be changed."

Perhaps he would have said more, but he saw the pain in his father's eyes. He laughed and changed the subject: "However, don't consider this an important desire, I too am very contented with my present life... And I am still young, perhaps if we arrange our affairs, there will also be time for this..."

Master Ali Riza seemed to believe his son.

They changed the subject and began to talk about something else.

Some of the pensioners in the café had found consolation in religion. Master Ali Riza's religion was to think of his son. From time to time when his hopelessness became insufferable, he bethought himself of Shevket, and he had the sensation of sitting down in the cool stillness of a temple.

One day, not hiding the tears in his eyes, he confessed this to Shevket: "My dear son, I thought I was an important man, I was foolishly proud. But I can't compare with you!"

Shevket was bewildered.

"What are you saying father... Can one imagine a man like you in the world? What is this childishness?" he said, laughing.

49

Master Ali Riza stubbornly shook his head. "I can't compare with you, my son. If you ask, 'Why?' it is because as long as I have been alive I felt nothing, wanted nothing... whereas you are a very sensitive child... You understand everything, you desire everything... You disappoint yourself by your very choice among what you want under the present circumstances. This is the difference between us, my child. It is because of this that you are at a much higher level than I am..."

XII

Little by little the children in the house began to quarrel. This was done at first in secret and Master Ali Riza didn't notice the true cause of it.

One day, Fikret scolded her sisters, the next day he heard Leila crying in her room, and on the third Nejla wouldn't come down to eat.

Mistress Hayriye had got herself into a totally unapproachable state, and Master Ali Riza didn't have the courage to ask her any questions because he knew with certainty that he would get a disagreeable answer.

Gradually the tumult grew. No one respected anyone else. At that time the old man saw that his children had divided into two camps: on one side, Fikret and on the other, Leila and Nejla.

This was a beautiful proof, showing that there was no father in the house who could make himself respected and obeyed.

Leila and Nejla didn't like the way in which their family lived; they wanted novelty, diversion and a few more things.

These two girls, in comparison to their other siblings, had grown up more flippant, coquettish and spoiled. Master Ali Riza had not taken much care of their education and thought. It was impossible that such pretty girls would be left alone for long. At the most, they would be gone in four or five years.

Master Ali Riza would say, "It's enough if Leila and Nejla grow up to be women of good reputation." The whole plan consisted of bringing them up in seclusion. He didn't permit them to go out very often, nor to be friends with anyone whose family wasn't known to be serious. He would continually order his wife: "At this age for children beauty is the greatest danger. Keep your eyes wide open!" But because he was afraid they would react badly to these constraints, he had flattered them excessively in the home. They had only to say one word, never two.

Recently, this had become the surface cause of a few quarrels with his wife. When Mistress Hayriye had complained that he was spending too much money on Leila and Nejla, he said, "Your opinion is not judicious, Mistress! We are secluding the girls at home... It's impossible not to give them what they want to wear and to eat. Afterwards, they would loathe the house, their life at home. If only we could possibly find a way to make them more happy at home!"

The first quarrel broke out between the girls, with Mistress Hayriye in the middle. The wretched woman held out for a while against the tears and weeping of Leila and Nejla. The serious Fikret tried secretly to help her mother in the last phase of the tumult. Afterwards, signs of weariness and defeat were seen in the old woman.

How could she bear to see her two grown children crying day and night? Mistress Hayriye began to scrimp on the most necessary expenses of the house for the sake of Leila and Nejla's toilette. At the end, little by little, her accounting began to collapse. This time Fikret criticized this weakness of her mother, and began by saying, "To make them happy, you have no right to make us suffer from poverty and ruin the household, mother!"

To defend herself, Mistress Hayriye was forced to defend Leila and Nejla as well; "They also are right... they want to dress like all the girls, they want elegance..."

Up until that time, Fikret had looked at her little sisters as her own children. This was a feeling that had been born and nurtured under the continual instruction of her father.

But really when her mother defended Leila and Nejla in this way, Fikret couldn't bear it.

"And what about us? Are we little animals, puppy dogs, mother? I'm not thinking of myself...But doesn't it wrong Aisha?" she said vehemently. A quarrel that until that time was pursued through suspended faces, secret swoons and recoveries, silent sobbing, broke out into the open. The factions separated, conflicts were joined. On one side were Leila, Nejla and Mistress Hayriye; on the other were Fikret and Aisha.

Only the two sides were not equal in strength. Because Aisha was very young, Fikret was considered to be alone. The young girl planned to get Shevket and Master Ali Riza on her side. Shevket said, after listening to his sister at length: "It isn't right for me to meddle in this matter, Fikret. They will say I'm throwing my weight around because my role is small in the household, it will seem hypocritical... But if I see a danger in the future, I won't remain silent!"

As for Master Ali Riza, it was quite clear that from now on he had begun to sink to the status of a garden scarecrow in the house. For him to meddle in this quarrel would have no result on the children other than the rolling of a hundred eyes. Now they considered him – to a degree – as a father. At that time, they would not consider him even necessary, just a broken down scarecrow under their feet.

For this reason, when Master Ali Riza heard shouts and voices beginning to be raised he would either go to his room and close the door, or else escape into the street by the kitchen door.

XIII

There was no observable difference in Master Ali Riza. But he saw and understood his children much better than in the old days.

Just as when in a serious illness, secret maladies of the body pop out into the open, this crisis had uncovered their defects and rotten spots.

52

Fikret and also the other girls were so different from what he had thought! The quarrel little by little changed its shape. Leila and Nejla spoke quite openly of their basic desires; by what right had they shut them up in the house? Instead of what everyone's daughter wanted, to go about and have fun with the people they wanted, why had they been sentenced to this hell?

The house's name from now on was "hell". And weren't they also young? To be with people, to go to parties, to dance, couldn't they want this? They thought their youth was passing by. What would be the end of this way of life? Had their father any plans for them? The house, like a ship whose hull has been pierced, was sinking day by day. In such times, didn't everyone have the right to save his own skin? The time of keeping them restrained was passing. Perhaps if they were left to their own devices, they would each find a suitable husband, they would save themselves. In such times, who would knock on their door and ask, "Do you have some daughters that need marrying?"

It was Spring. Friday and Sunday a procession of men and women would pass in front of their door, going to country dance parties in the woods opposite. When the girls heard the gramophone they would go mad, the inside of the house would be stirred up.

Fikret began the assault with a force that couldn't be anticipated from her puny body and serious nature. "It's a matter of the family honor. Should dances and society and I don't know what else come into Master Ali Riza's house? My father and brother would never accept it."

Mistress Hayriye couldn't defend Leila and Nejla on this point. But she attacked their father who was opposed to it: "I am not content for my daughters to be thrown and scattered about, but what can we do, it's their father's fault. He has insisted on a course of righteousness. We have not a handful, not even something to grasp between two fingers, in this manner of living the children are afraid of not finding a husband, and they are right."

Master Ali Riza was naturally content with this obstinacy of his oldest daughter. But he understood very well that Fikret wasn't struggling just for the sake of the family honor. From now on, he had also learned to understand her. These fits of temper of his oldest girl were only the result of jealousy, of the fact that she didn't possess her sisters' beauty. And it was this way, not only now, but in the old days too. Fikret of old had dominated her sisters with seriousness, good behavior, and knowledge. But now their years had advanced. What is more, because of the daily progression of age and poverty, the influence of seriousness, good behavior, and knowledge in the home had diminished. Now the family had left no other coppers than their beauty. If Leila and Nejla spoke freely and openly, they would place the value of their wretched older sister, so plain of countenance, at zero.

Master Ali Riza's thought, "I erred in Fikret's education," from now on wouldn't change.

Like everything, the work he had expended educating his children was wasted effort. Whatever there was in the leaven of their lineage, at the moment of their birth, was becoming evident as time passed, nothing could have changed it.

In spite of this belief, in one hour or another of peace and hope, he would go to Nejla and Leila and begin to tell them all the things that were burning up his heart. Oh, if it had been possible to explain himself even a little bit to these children! Unfortunately, this was impossible. He wouldn't have succeeded in making them hear his voice, no matter how much he shouted. These heads that were near enough to touch with his hand were strange worlds farther than the farthest stars.

During these hours, Master Ali Riza looked at his daughters like sacrificial lambs: his heart wept blood.

XIV

Gehenna – hell -- the first ones he caught using that word were Leila and Nejla. Now the whole family, even little Aisha, was calling the house "gehenna".

But this gehenna had a half hour truce every day: the evening meals… In the space of a half hour, the cries and the tears stopped, in the dining room an air of peace and friendship reminiscent of the old days was manufactured. The cause of this miracle was Shevket. For whatever reason, the whole family continued to love and respect him. This was perhaps because he hadn't gotten mixed up in the quarrels. Or also because they were weary of squabbling and tearing one another to pieces from morning to night.

All the expressions changed the moment he sat down at the table, while he continued to eat, everyone spoke quite nicely to one another. But after a time, there was a change even in Shevket. It was as if he had lost his old gaiety and liveliness. While he was talking and laughing at the table like old times, sometimes he would bury his chin in his hands, plunged in thought.

Master Ali Riza at first thought that the paleness in his color and the shadows in his golden eyes were the result of the evening and the bad light given off by the petrol lamp.

But his child's manner of speech had also changed. Whenever he said hopeful things with a passionate, emotional voice, suddenly he would stop as if he were worn out, and become pessimistic without any cause. Perhaps the boy works too hard? A few times he wanted to broach this fear with his wife but hadn't had the courage. Mistress Hayriye had become an unapproachable woman.

If she perceived the perplexity of her husband, she would say something contrary out of pure spite and make him confused. But Mistress Hayriye would recover first.

One Winter evening, Master Ali Riza was dozing at the head of the brazier, a book in his hand. Mistress Hayriye asked as she cracked the door open: "Haven't you already gone to bed?" Then she came inside.

With a hypocritical expression, she said: "The room is very cold... Don't you feel cold?"

She poked the brazier. She stuffed paper into a crack in a window that let in a breeze. Then she looked at the places where Master Ali Riza's galabia[5] had come unstitched.

"Take that off and give it to me, I'll sew it up."

But seeing her husband give her the galabia and remain in his flannel night shirt, she was afraid that he would get cold, and taking the blanket from the cushion she threw it over his shoulders.

Master Ali Riza didn't take these courtesies as a good omen. His wife's stealthy hovering, her showing him a sweetness that amounted to replacing her previous peevishness and contrariness with abject fawning, would not be without a purpose. He thought of servants that they had used when times were good. Mistress Hayriye would continually ill use and torment these women. But one day she suddenly changed her manner. What kindness, what courtesy, what delicacy! That evening the servants saw the treatment of an honored guest. And that's what they really were... Because the next morning they found that she had absolutely decided to put a bundle in their hands and turn them out of the house.

Thus Master Ali Riza understood that this evening she was going to ask a big sacrifice of him.

---

[5] A loose outer garment.

After the old woman had labored over her sewing for two minutes, she said "Master Ali Riza, there's something important I have to speak with you about, I don't know what to do. I've just come from Shevket's room. We spoke for a long long time…"

The old man waited for the end with the bewildered resignation of an invalid who is about to be put on the operating table.

After making an inexhaustible and unending preamble as if she wanted to prolong his torment, his wife said: "Our son loves a woman and wants absolutely to marry her."

Shevket was very young. He was of the age when men believe there is nothing more serious and important in the world than love. Even though Master Ali Riza knew this very well, he was quite incapable of believing his wife. In his opinion, love was an affliction that some men brought on their own head knowingly and willingly, a construct of free time that got in the way of work. How could Shevket, so passionate about his work, so serious and intelligent, have committed such an insanity?

After Master Ali Riza had thought at length, he twisted his neck around. "What can we do if he wants to get married? He has the right… No one can be forced to sacrifice…"

Mistress Hayriye agreed with him: "You are right about this. Only there is something else that makes me think a little… I don't know what you'll say."

"You said there's something more? Why are you beating around the bush, say it!"

"You're old… I'm afraid of worrying you too much."

Master Ali Riza began to shake. Suddenly Mistress Hayriye was hesitant to trouble him too much. This was Mistress Hayriye who for a time had taken pleasure in every opportunity to make him writhe. That meant that he was going to hear something inconceivably fearful and bitter. The old man tried to hide his apprehension: "Don't worry, out with it, from now on I'm used to everything..."

The woman finished her sewing, she bent over the top of the brazier, opposite her husband, and said as she raked the ashes with the tongs: "Shevket fell in love with a typist in the bank... She was a married woman... For a time they met secretly... Finally the affair was discovered... The woman was thrown out by her husband... Now she can't go to the bank because of her shame... If she doesn't marry Shevket, she says she'll commit suicide..."

Master Ali Riza didn't get all aflutter as his wife expected. Rather, in his state and appearance there was a deep peace. He said, smiling with profound bitterness: "Does Shevket want to marry this woman?"

"Yes if you consent. You could save two souls at once..."

"Shevket from now on is a grown up man... Thus it is natural, he can do whatever he wants... But as for me, I could never consent to this marriage..."

"What are you saying, Master Ali Riza?"

"The words of a real man, wife... If my son does something like this, I will consider him dead... I had one son, God took him from me, my speech is stopped up, my eyes are crusted over... Unfortunately, there is nothing to be done..."

Mistress Hayriye knew her husband, she knew well that whatever she said on this matter would have no effect. For that reason, without saying anything more, as she sat, she began to cry without making a sound.

Master Ali Riza said with the same calm: "It's useless to cry, Mistress, let me repeat, I will never take this woman into my house. If Shevket doesn't obey me, if he says, 'It's I who support this household... What right do you have to say anything?', then the matter changes. I won't see any of you any more, I'll take myself elsewhere, I'll go away. You can tell my son what I've said... I'm not angry with you... But what can I do, there is no way I can do anything else."

58

Mistress Hayriye left the room in tears. Because Master Ali Riza understood that he wouldn't sleep that night, he didn't come to bed but stayed by the brazier and thought until morning, wrapped in the blanket.

XV

Again the house was divided into two camps. Fikret was powerfully opposed to this marriage. For one thing, the woman who would enter among them as a sister-in-law was suspect because she had had passed through many adventures. Then, the total penury and tightness of money in the house would increase.

As for Leila and Nejla, they highly favored Shevket's marriage. Whatever happened, along with this woman a little novelty and diversion would come into the house. Under the influence of his wife, Shevket who had the head of an old man like his father, would absolutely have to change.

A powerful struggle between the two camps began. On this subject, Master Ali Riza remained hard as granite. Moreover, Fikret became an unexpectedly powerful comrade in arms.

But Mistress Hayriye didn't lose hope that she would conquer her husband; although she wasn't discovered attacking openly, she endeavored to wear him down bit by bit with a secret stratagem: since they had the money and power in their own hands, sooner or later they would overcome the stubbornness of this senseless old man. But there was only one thing: "Shevket acts too weak. Ah, the one who can hardly stand up to his father, could he be a man in strength? What use is it for such a big youth to do nothing else but weep secret tears and pine away day by day, like a girl? It seems as if nothing has changed between the father and his son. Shevket continually shows more deference to his father, he proves by his manner and his words that he won't offend him, whatever the price."

"Shevket, I really don't want you to disobey your father, but at least you could show your displeasure!" she would counsel him.

"Mother, you don't know how much I understand and love this man... Don't be angry or offended... I love you too very much... But my love for him is something totally different, almost like a type of worship."

At first, Mistress Hayriye tried to trick and soften her husband by using his crazy love for Shevket. She explained at length that if this marriage didn't happen their son would either die or commit suicide. As a matter of fact, she could see the old father in a state of collapse lying by the deathbed of his son; his hands over his eyes, he was weeping soundlessly, but at the end he would say with an unshakable belief that death was infinitely preferable to this marriage.

One day when Shevket seemed particularly distraught, there was a fearsome scene between the husband and wife. Mistress Hayriye, writhing in the grip of a powerful nervous crisis, began to scream "I won't let you kill your son before my eyes!"

Master Ali Riza responded in tears: "Very well, don't be upset... Let Shevket do what he wants... Don't think of me. I'll leave... You won't even hear my name any more."

The woman wrapped herself around his neck and began to scream with even more force: "How dare you say this! Do you understand that a husband with a family who escapes and leaves a wretched woman with a bunch of children is worse than a common thief?"

This scene proved to Mistress Hayriye that all her strength was in vain. A little more excitement would have killed the old man, but wouldn't have changed one atom of his opinion. That was when she changed her strategy.

Since her husband considered this marriage a disgrace, in that case she would prove to him that on the contrary for his son to abandon this wretched woman was a greater disgrace. Mistress Hayriye for a time attacked him from this direction: "Your son has destroyed the honor of a family, by leaving a pitiable woman in the street. One soul is worth

60

another… That wretch is a child like your Fikret, like the inexperienced Leila and Nejla… Afterwards God will take from us one of our own children. It is incumbent on your son to restore the honor of this woman."

At the time, Master Ali Riza appeared not to heed this argument. But underneath this rock, apparently immoveable, several unseen pieces of debris had collected.

One day for no reason he called his wife to his side and said with quiet resignation: "Mistress, I have thought at length. It would not be right for our son to abandon this woman… Tell Shevket from me… We are prepared to receive the woman he wants, to open our arms to her as one of our children."

XVI

The evening of the wedding… The house was bathed in light to the rafters… Doors and windows had been thrown open. One or two jazz bands were playing. In moments of silence, merry peals of laughter, shouts, screams...

In the street there was a secret life like the swarming of nighttime bugs gathered around a powerful light… a crowd that had flowed from far and wide straight to the music and light. Women, men, children… Some were looking at the happiness of the marriage house in the street, others were slowly and cautiously approaching the garden, taking courage from the doors that had been thrown wide open because of the confusion inside.

They were sitting on the edges of the flower beds that Master Ali Riza had tended so carefully.

Children, even adults, were seen dancing with the jazz band's music… Master Ali Riza quietly escaped behind the kitchen door, and went to a hill four or five hundred paces distant.

He sat on the edge of a big rock, resting his beard in his hands. In this state, he looked like a wretch who was watching his house go up in flames from a distance. From now on, no hope remained in his face. How heroically he had struggled for long years, with closed doors and desolate dark windows in Bağlarbaşı, against the strength, increasing day by day, of the tempest outside his house! This useless resistance had cost him so many tears and deprivations.

This marriage was like a strong gust of wind that blew down the doors in a moment, all the old man's fears had suddenly invaded the house.

Yes, now his hopes were finished. With Shevket, he had lost his most powerful comrade in arms, and he was totally alone in the world.

For weeks, Master Ali Riza had lived like someone whose feet were heavy. But on this evening when everything was over, he found the time to remember the things he had seen and to think with a clear head.

The children had chattered openly of the wedding and even the serious Fikret, had pestered him about clothes. He couldn't expect help from his wife, nor from Shevket. It was around that wretched child's head that the flames were burning.

Master Ali Riza for a time had tried to explain to each one of his deeply bewildered children in different ways that this marriage was not an occasion of joy and pride as they thought... Somehow it had come into being to repair a calamity; rather than shouting the shame that had fallen on themselves from the housetops with fife and drums, as much as possible it should pass in silence.

And even if this weren't so, what could they use to provide the clothes and the wedding? They had nothing at all left.

If they took it into their heads to go into debt, things would totally get out of control, a few months later they would really be hungry and would be an object of scorn to the world.

The old man one day bewildered Aisha, he went through account books

62

for hours will this eleven year old baby, showing her grocery receipts, promissory notes, documents. But from now on the children too gave him no respect. Now each one was a little Mistress Hayriye. They would cry with the exact expression their mother had when she was angry, "Really what's a man like you good for? You didn't think of us. You did worse than your beggar children. When most people don't take two seconds when their children say one, won't you be ashamed to make us walk about like servants at our brother's wedding?"

Master Ali Riza was a philosopher. He suspected that anything could happen to a human being. But he had never conceived the idea that the nail to be driven into the head of reputation and uprightness, such a great shame and unimaginable disgrace, would come from his children. But the disease didn't only consist in talking about clothes. The household chattels were also totally changed. The old broken furniture, the bedsteads, the tables, the armchairs were sold, new ones came in their place, they wallpapered some of the rooms.

These were things that cost money. Master Ali Riza didn't have the courage even to imagine what Shevket was doing, what he was withdrawing to affront all these expenditures. A few times however he tried to talk to his son. But from now on Shevket would turn away without meeting his eyes, would bend his head with a desperate and guilty expression, and saying, "I know, father... But it was necessary," would escape.

Mistress Hayriye had poured out whatever there was in her basket and coffer, and brought the last one or two emeralds to auction. But all this didn't make anyone in the house happy, every evening loud screams would break out, there would be fainting spells and recoveries, Mistress Hayriye, not considering Master Ali Riza a man who had money to spend, would pester her husband whenever her head was troubled, saying: "Tell me, aren't you the man of the house? I'm just a weak women... What can I do?... Find a way..."

The worst side of the business was that Master Ali Riza couldn't stand to see his daughter-in-law, Ferhunde. He remembered the day he had first seen her. The old man thought that he was going to meet a wretched woman, bashful and humble, weeping from love that he had accepted her into a good family and had cleaned her reputation. But on the contrary he discovered a spoiled, flighty and insolent creature who looked down from a great height and saw inexhaustible rights in herself.

There were some words that he would have said to this woman about the happiness of his son and the honor of the family. But when he saw with one glance that she was a person he couldn't talk to, he gave up and made no plans other than leaving himself to events.

*

**

As the jazz band played without stopping, he saw a crowd of people leaping and kicking up their heels behind the windows whose lattices had been thrown open two days ago.

Master Ali Riza thought about Mistress Hayriye. She was now downstairs in the kitchen, working among piles of dirty dishes in the dim light of a torch, forced to work preparing hors d'oeuvres for the drinks. For a long time, Master Ali Riza had been angry at this woman who had left him alone at his most difficult hour. But nevertheless this evening he was sorry for her.

This tiny woman, what hadn't she borne to bring up these five children? At a time when a man will sit peacefully in a corner, taking a sigh of relief, his job finished, was it right for her to be all flustered and working, exhausting herself with the daily struggle?

Certainly she also wasn't pleased with the way things were, she couldn't be…

It was impossible for a pure housewife who had passed her life among four walls, never seeing a human face except for her children, to change suddenly. Perhaps it was necessary to seek the cause of this change in her excessive love for these children. Whatever the case was, she was an

64

unthinking, simple woman. Her poor head had not permitted her to see her future, she was motivated only by sensations, the sensations of a slender mother who wanted to prevent at whatever cost the wailing of her children. For the sake of a few things that she should have found repulsive, only because they wanted them, because it was absolutely necessary to make them happy, for this reason she hadn't shrunk from mistreating her husband of many years. Yes the two of them probably loved their children equally, what a shame it was that this love took different directions!

In his heart Master Ali Riza was also a little disappointed in Shevket, but this evening he was forgiving to him as well and he felt that he was sorry for his child's madness. That day they had crossed paths a few times. Although he hadn't looked very carefully, he saw that his son was bewildered and in despair. His beautiful intelligent head was as pale as beeswax in his bridegroom suit.

Once when they were alone, he had approached Master Ali Riza: "Father, can you listen to me for a bit?" he had said. But his voice had suddenly turned to tears, and using as pretext that someone had called him from upstairs, he had escaped.

I wonder what the child had wanted to say? Master Ali Riza didn't know. But he thought that if they had talked now at this hour, in these very different places, the two of them would have been more cheerful and less pessimistic.

XVII

Leila and Nejla were not mistaken in their conjectures.

Their sister-in-law was an open-minded, daring woman.

Already when she was talking with them on the day of the marriage, she seemed to smell something. "In this house, there's a smell like a tomb," she had said. "In my opinion, you must open the windows and doors, change the air a little. I don't know, perhaps because you are used to it you don't smell it."

The girls had raised their heads to the heavens with a beautiful sad expression that would have made a movie star jealous. They didn't smell anything? You, or anyone, could ask them. The wretched children were really in their death throes from lake of breath, like birds caught on a spit who have emptied out their air. But what could they do? Their father was an old fashioned man, their mother was a bitter woman. There was a staidness that had caught their big sister, Fikret. In spite of her twenty years, she exceeded her father in being old fashioned. As for Shevket... Somehow or other, up until now they hadn't seen his modern and diverting side.

Thank God under the influence of their sister-in-law, he too was opening up a little, he was becoming like "modern young men" of his age. But from that wretch they got nothing more then shared tears.

They trusted their sister-in-law so much on the very first day that they poured out into Ferhunde's heart, with their moist eyes open and tears scattered about, their real desire to be helped by her. The young woman said, kissing Leila and Nejla's hair, "You poor innocents! How can these beautiful eyes bear to cry? Don't worry. From now on, we've become three. Somehow we'll make our pain understood."

When Ferhunde said, "We've become three," it was nothing but false modesty. Really, from this day, she made quite clear that she was the most powerful member of the new party in the house and the main mast.

66

This young woman was as daring and tricky as she was intelligent. Within a few days, she took control and began to govern the house as its one and only head.

Master Ali Riza, who until now had walked around the house like a ghost, disappeared altogether. Early in the morning he would go out into the street, and would pass the day walking around by himself in the countryside or sitting in the cafés.

A division had opened up between Fikret and her father, and the young girl, not wanting to converse with her sister-in-law and her sisters, shut herself up all day long in her room with a savage stubbornness.

In her opinion, the responsibility for everything that was happening lay with Master Ali Riza. If he hadn't neglected his duties as head of the family, if he had ruled with the firmness befitting a strong man, would they have been reduced in this way?

The young girl didn't neglect telling her thoughts to Master Ali Riza. Sometimes when they were alone, she would prick her father mercilessly: "It doesn't matter to me... Whatever happens, my life is broken... But I'm sorry for Aisha... The poor little lamb will grow up without morals among these people..." she would say, driving her father totally insane.

In Master Ali Riza's opinion, Fikret wasn't completely wrong. He too was somewhat responsible for this business. There were two big sins: the first was, that he was refined. The second was that being without money was an even more unpardonable crime.

The old man had to admit that the words his wife said when he left "Goldleaf Limited" were justified.

"Did you do well to leave the company? What did others' immorality have to do with you? At any rate, you could have saved yourself from shame and your family from this danger."

One evening the old man begged his wife to iron his clothes. He dressed with great care, like in the old days. When his wife wanted to know the reason for this elegance, he answered vaguely, saying: "Nothing... I want to visit an old friend."

He intended to look like this to pay his respects to the director of "Goldleaf limited," Master Muzaffer. Perhaps his old student would give him some work.

But there was his oath never to see Muzaffer face to face. But this was a resolution of ancient times and of the old Master Ali Riza.

It wasn't that he had softened toward the sin that his own son had committed; but from now on, to criticize, to stand up and discourse about upright conduct in a loud voice, would have been ridiculous.

Master Ali Riza first stopped by the secretarial office, and found that several of his friends weren't there any more. The others almost seemed to have trouble recognizing him. The old man spent as long as possible in the corridor, and after reading line by line the notices posted there, went to the director's office. Somehow his hands were shaking as if he were committing a great crime, he completely lacked the courage to enter and knock at the door.

Perhaps he would have waited longer in the corridor, gathering up his strength, reading the notices one more time, but suddenly the door opened. Master Muzaffer came out holding a full satchel.

"My teacher!! Is it you?... What is it? Are you well, by God?"

The young man seemed not to be surprised to find him hanging out so guiltily by his door. Master Ali Riza's heart was suddenly twisted up: "Thank God, sir, I came to see you... Some business of mine took me today in this direction..."

Master Muzaffer interrupted: "You didn't want to miss the occasion to ask after me? I thank you... How are you?... By God you don't seem changed. How is your son? And your daughters are well, by God? Surely by now they must have grown up!"

68

Master Muzaffer piled one question on top of another as if he wanted to finish the necessary courtesies as quickly as possible, meanwhile searching through his satchel and looking at the papers in it. He said to a lackey waiting with a stick and beret in his hand: "My son, there is a sealed envelope on the table... Bring it to me."

Then he shook Master Ali Riza's hand: "My teacher, excuse me! I must leave on an urgent matter. I'm happy that our paths crossed and you dropped in... Good bye!"

Leaving the old man in the corridor, he descended the staircase at speed.

Thus this last hope had fallen into the water.

XVIII

Now Leila and Nejla got their wish. At last they had arrived at the "modern living" they desired for years.

Master Ali Riza rose and went to bed amidst a crazy gaiety and merriment, as if his old and broken down house in Bağlarbaşı itself wanted to throw off the bitterness of its deprivations.

Two evenings a week they gave a tea party with dancing for guests, at least two or three evenings in addition they would go to parties given by others. They removed the glass case in the downstairs anteroom and courtyard and covered the pierced rotten walls with yellow starred wallpaper. For the evening parties, they would take the water jug, the dining table and other rubbishy furniture to the kitchen, and bring down kilims, armchairs and elegant pillows from upstairs to create the décor of a reception room.

In their flurry, there was often no time to prepare dinner or eat.

Everyone would take one or two biscuits or a sandwich from the table prepared for the guests, to be eaten standing and in haste. A little later, when the guests would appear one by one, Mistress Hayriye would gather up her skirts and roll up her sleeves, retreating to the kitchen for buffet duty, while Master Ali Riza, so as to hear the tumult downstairs as little as possible, would go to the attic with a book in his sleeve and a candle in his hand.

The gramophone would play all evening, they danced without stopping amidst crazy mad shouting, and, as if the house were being shaken from its foundations, dust would rain from the ruined ceilings...

Most of the time, Master Ali Riza would fall asleep where he sat in front of the dwindling candle, and when he opened his eyes in the morning's first light, he would discover the house still being shaken by this tumult.

As for the evenings when the family went out, this time because of the inexhaustible endless preparations, there was also no time for the evening meal. The girls and their sister-in-law would sew up stitches for hours and make elegant creations out of the remnants of ruined dresses, anointing the bare places of their bodies with cologne and painting themselves in front of the mirror like chanteuses.

It seemed that the peevishness and captiousness that affected all the big and little people of the house had also infected Master Ali Riza.

Now and then the old man blew his stack, and began to scream and yell that he wouldn't permit this scandalous behavior, at which time, wherever Mistress Hayriye was, she would arrive running, and scold him: "Are you crazy, Master Ali Riza? Whatever we do, it's going to be this way... It's necessary for the girls to find husbands... We have done this only for them to find a suitable match... You've made your children rich, let them alone to take care of their wretched heads..."

Apparently Shevket was also of this opinion. "Papa, life has changed," he would say. "Believe that this diversion is not to be feared as you think... Now everybody does this... What can we do... We're forced to conform to the requirements of modernity... Because you are a man of another time, you don't see how normal and necessary these things are."

At first, Master Ali Riza was bewildered, and thought that his son too had changed like the other children, been spoiled. But a little after he understood that Shevket was still the old Shevket.

None of his thoughts and feelings had changed at all. He too was not happy with these goings-on, he liked neither this life style, nor people coming and going in their house; but what could he do when the matter had come off the rails, once he was caught in this fearsome current, either because of his weak spot for his wife or for other reasons.

When his son was speaking, wasn't this shown by his desperate and troubled expression? Yes, Shevket was still the old Shevket. Such things neither this time or at any time could he think natural and necessary. What could he do, when the arrow had already left the bow.

After Master Ali Riza had come to this conclusion, he began to be much more sorry for his son.

The child seemed day by day to have become drugged and wasted away. After evenings of death inviting partying, very often without sleeping he would take his pouch and go out into the street, fighting and quarreling who knew where and how, returning after nightfall in a state of weary exhaustion. But, although anyone who saw him would know he was sick to the point of needing bed rest, nevertheless without even taking a moment to rest and eat with his wife, they would go out and add more evening parties to the earlier ones. Mistress Hayriye was still the manager. But the wretched woman had now truly lost hold of the end of the rope. In the house they were spending money like water. Where did this money come from? Did Shevket earn enough to handle this fearsome expenditure even at the expense of working himself to death? Or was the wretched boy drowning in debts?

XIX

A few months passed after the wedding. The fountain of money that had seemed to flow in the early days like water without accounting or bookkeeping started to dry up. Then the season of arguments came back.

Shevket seemed to be in deep difficulty. Some mornings he would escape without leaving his mother any money for expenses, sometimes he told them to tell creditors at the door that he wasn't in. Again the family fell upon one another, some days Ferhunde would be screaming from nerves; other days Leila and Nejla thought of committing suicide, other days it was Aisha who was crying.

Unlike her husband, Mistress Hayriye for her part amidst these quarrels was always running from one to another, entreating, trying to find a compromise.

They had reached the ultimate degree of poverty. There were some days without fire in the house, without hot food. Everyone besides Ferhunde, who had a secret stash of jam and dry sardines in her cupboard, filled his belly in a corner with what was at hand, olives, cheese, pastrami,[6] in very cold weather they would wrap themselves in quilts without covers.

However when the party days came, again everything changed. The whole house presented a peaceful appearance, faces smiled, they began trying to cooperate. Someone carried in the dining table and prepared the reception room, someone else did the sewing and repaired stocking heels, another did the ironing, Aisha used an old hole punch to make colored kites into confetti.

As for Mistress Hayriye, she again rolled up her sleeves and went into the kitchen, and she would slice stale rolls and make sandwiches filled with margarine or pieces of cheese. The poor woman was as expert in this work as a deli clerk. She would make real caviar by mixing a spoonful of black caviar with olives and sardine guts, and liquors by

---

[6] Turkish pastirma, a kind of pressed meat.

means of boiling bad fruit to which she added glasses of wine left over from old parties.

One day, first thing in the morning, they were fighting hair to hair, head to head, the next laughing and having fun they would paint each other's nails, pluck their eyebrows with tweezers, and sit sewing.

One of the things that Master Ali Riza didn't understand, was that, writhing and eating one another amidst the most bitter poverty, when party time came, they would forget everything and begin to laugh and have fun as if nothing had happened.

It was clear that his children had lost their feeling and dignity, as if they were gypsies.

When Master Ali Riza wanted to say something, an answer was ready-made: "What can we do, it's none of our business... It's necessary for the girls to find husbands..."

Moreover, with this pretext, Mistress Hayriye began to send Master Ali Riza out to meet the guests: "Go out in public rather than skulking in the attic like a weasel. Among the people who come and go in the house, there are people who want Leila and Nejla. Aren't you their father? You are the one who will have the last word. Speak with these men, try to get to know their morals and temperaments."

Master Ali Riza didn't think these words were totally mistaken. This was no time to be cross and withdraw into a corner. Whatever happened, Leila and Nejla were his daughters. Since there were people coming and going in the house who had thoughts of getting married with them, he should absolutely choose two reputable men among them. At this point, he saw no other means of preventing harm from happening to his children. Master Ali Riza would endure this misfortune for the sake of his children.

From now on, in the evenings when there were parties, he too made his preparations in a corner like an actor about to make his entrance in the play. He would touch up his shoe color, use scissors to cut threads

73

hanging down from his pant legs, take great care pushing the torn parts of his shirt underneath his tie, comb out his hair and beard.

When Master Ali Riza came in, with the serious demeanor he had adopted when he entered the director's office at the school, the girls, fresh from their sequined and beaded toilettes, would rush at him shaking their bare arms like wings, and crying with a spoiled voice: "Daddykins... Darling little daddykins," they would wrap their arms around him and sit him down in an armchair. They would bring biscuits and sandwiches and make every effort to stuff them into his mouth.

As for the guests, what a disgusting deceit this was. Master Ali Riza compared his daughters to theater girls who, first pushed and shoved into the wings by the old actor, begin to smell and to kiss – whatever the role calls for – when the curtain opens, and he was disgusted both by them and by himself. What could he do, he was forced to suffer this as well. Perhaps he would hunt down a husband for his children at these parties by means of play acting the bourgeois family. The only thing was that among these heaps and heaps of men coming and going in the house, he didn't see even one countenance that resembled a man. They were ignorant, uneducated, impertinent neighborhood children of nineteen or twenty years old... All kinds of vagabonds who discoursed with a amazing lack of shame, some about gambling, others about women, about big maneuvers in business or the stock market, or about big inheritances they had either consumed or were waiting for... Wasted, drug addled, swollen, alcoholic faces... Old foxes thrusting their way into families for the sole purpose of seducing their innocent daughters...

Master Ali Riza sat crouched down in a corner, as if he noticed nothing, but he was looking inside these faces, and as his daughters were speaking and joking familiarly with them, he was dying of shame.

Shevket's condition in these assemblies was absolutely the same. It was plain that this wretched child lived in pain and torment. But what use was it, he totally couldn't free himself from the trap when once it had been sprung. Shevket wouldn't have suffered Master Ali Riza to go out among the guests. Sometimes when their eyes met, he would twist his neck as if

74

saying, "I brought you to this state, forgive me!"

One evening the young man brought his father outside on a pretext, and bending down to his ear in the hallway said, "Dear father, if you have pity on me, don't be among these men," and without waiting for an answer, he escaped.

XX

Fikret was living by herself in a room on the top floor of the house, coming out only once in a while to quarrel, but one evening she asked her father to come in. She said, without preamble, "Father, I'm getting married."

Master Ali Riza was surprised, but he didn't show any anxiety. "Really, my child? May God grant you happiness."

"Maybe you are angry with me for taking such a decision without consulting you…"

Master Ali Riza answered with a bitter smile: "Angry? Why should I be angry, my child? I have no right over you, because…"

Fikret knitted her brows: "It's not right to reproach me this way, father."

"I'm not reproaching you… I'm telling you the truth… I've become a pauper… I've lost my rights as a father like all my other rights… Since I'm not capable of providing for your happiness… My child, you have the right to do whatever you want…"

For the first time, Fikret was a little upset, as if she was sorry for her father. But her face became severe again, and she said with a serious and hesitant expression: "Let me speak openly, father. You know that I'm not such a very thoughtless girl. At no time did it cross my mind to be angry with you like my mother and sisters that we became poor and without money. The weakness that you showed for them and against me, I pardoned although I wouldn't have done it. Shevket isn't a bad child. But

75

what use is it, when he has given his bridle to that worthless woman. Leila and Nejla are two madwomen who don't know what they have done... My mother is a wretch who goes like a lamb wherever she's pulled... I struggled and struggled, saying 'Father open your eyes, they're dragging the family down to its ruin.' You paid me no mind. I withdrew into a corner like a stranger, you were content with only getting angry and sour faced... If you had acted like a man, these things would have been impossible. Perhaps you'll be sad, but that doesn't make it necessary to hide the reality that's in plain sight... This conduct isn't good conduct... We are going straight for the precipice at full gallop... There's no help from anyone that I can see... I said, 'Let me save myself at least.' That's why it wouldn't be unreasonable for you get angry and say 'Why is this girl doing this thing without asking once?' "

Master Ali Riza sat on the edge of a chest and said, as his hand held his head where not a single black hair remained: "You are right, Fikret, my child, I am the cause of all this."

The father and daughter said for a while facing one another and thinking. Then Master Ali Riza began to ask questions: "At least is the man you are going to marry a good man, Fikret?"

"He is a fifty year old man named Master Tahsin..."

"Isn't that too old for you?"

"Very suitable for a creature like me..."

"What work does he do?"

"He's retired but has got vineyards and orchards in Adapazar..."

"Is he taking you there?"

"It's really because of that that I want him..."

"Has he already been married?"

"His wife died last year... They had three children..."

76

"What kind of man is he?"

"Not bad, they say... For my own account, I didn't even want to see a picture."

"Yes, but what if you don't like him?"

"To escape from this hell I would have been willing to take anybody."

"Did he ask for you by a go-between?"

With a broken off nervous laugh, Fikret said: "Naturally it wasn't a go-between who sent for me when she heard of my virtues from afar, saying 'For God's sake get this rare Indian fabric for me.' This man was a relative of our neighbor Mistress Neyyir... This man came to Istanbul recently and said, 'Since my wife's death the house is topsy-turvy. If I find a poor good girl who would be willing to be a mother to my children, I'll get married.' Without any hesitation whatsoever, I said, 'Take me.' They wrote a letter; yesterday the answer came... In two weeks, I'll be going to Adapazar.

While Fikret was giving this explanation with a peevish and bitter expression, her small tears made Master Ali Riza think of the dreams she had dreamed. He couldn't restrain himself from saying, "Oh my poor child!"

The young girl raised her head ill-temperedly and said with a savage anger, "Father, you would do better to save your mercy for your other children, until we see how they'll turn out."

Two weeks after, as she had said, Fikret went to Adapazar. Mistress Hayriye turned her cupboards inside out for the last time, trying to find two or three bits of stuff for her daughter, but the young girl gave them back with contempt. Likewise she didn't allow anyone from her family to accompany her to Adapazar...

"I'm leaving this family like a servant... Ceremonies aren't necessary."

When the day came, she allowed only her father and Aisha to go with her to the Haydarpasha station.

When she left the house, she didn't take leave of her sisters, and, with a nervous gesture, she pushed her mother, who was weeping and wanted to embrace her, down from her chest...

Only when the train began to move, did she seem to be slightly aware of the mute and hopeless sorrow in her father's eyes. Bending down from the carriage window, she said, "Don't give up hope, daddy. If you're really in trouble you can come to me... I'll look after you like my own child."

In this way, one of the tree's leaves broke off and fell down.

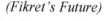

(Fikret's Future)

XXI

Master Ali Riza had only one hope left.

To get rid of Leila and Nejla by finding each one a suitable mate without any delay.

If the pretext of finding husbands for the girls disappeared, then perhaps also the immoral conduct would end. Although he knew that the real mischief was caused by his daughter-in-law Ferhunde, he figured the business would get somewhat easier when she lost her helpers and was alone.

At this point, the old man prepared the speeches he would make to Shevket: "My dear son... I love you as of old... If I were anything but an old man thrown on the dung heap, if I were considered the head of the family... My duties haven't yet finished... This state of affairs cannot continue... Despite everything, you are a good and industrious man... If you could make a little effort, I would hope that you could explain my purpose to your wife... If you have some weakness for her or if there is some reason this is impossible, we will take away our children... I no longer want anything from you... I'll support your mother and Aisha somehow on my monthly pension of a few piastres.

After Master Ali Riza had spoken, he would put an end to the parties and diversions, and close his door again. If his wife took it into her head to oppose him, he put it into his head to sacrifice her. Supposing that Mistress Hayriye didn't want to obey him, he would go and live with each of his children in turn.

The disaster had won Master Ali Riza something precious, opposite to the type of thing he had got rid of: brazenness, cunning...

He was no longer the old fearful shy government servant who split hairs and couldn't decide to pursue something important without thinking it over and shilly-shallying.

As he had become accustomed bit by bit to jawing in the street with tradesmen for a few piastres, so too had he grown used to arguing with his family in the house.

Of old when things were really intolerable, when he believed he was absolutely right, he couldn't yell and scream. Now he had become someone who wound everything around his finger for no cause at all, who boiled whoever was in front of him with the stubbornness of a child.

Perhaps what had a big share in this was the fact that his health was deteriorating day by day.

Yes, events had made Master Ali Riza into a totally different man. When the day came, he clearly understood that he wouldn't be helpless, as in the old days, to defend his right and his beliefs. The fact was that God would show at that time…

Only among the men who prowled around the girls, coming and going continually in the house, it didn't seem such an easy thing at all to find those two "well brought up" sons-in-law.

From now on, Master Ali Riza went about among the guests he hadn't summoned, at times he didn't want, seeking, like Diogenes in the street with a lamp in broad daylight, those two saviors who relied on the guidance of morality.

Among those who came and went, a few men, with whom he had chatted amicably, took on prison eye after a period of weeks. He invented pretexts to talk with them. He made secret researches into their lives. But in the end no one survived any sort of scrutiny.

It was also not necessary to be much of a soothsayer to tell how little the surface of these men resembled the inside. If you poked them a little with the finger tip, the superficial gilding would come off and you would see red loathsome wounds full of dirt and immorality. Master Ali Riza compared some of them to the house itself, to the reception room, to his own daughters. His girls would walk around the house by day clad in their mother's torn jacket, old cloaks that were good for nothing other than being kitchen rags; they unwillingly took up needles to sew up torn

80

and rent places in garments that had changed color from dirt and concealed them over and over with pieces of fabric. But on party nights, with rouge and spangled silk gowns, they left their cocoons and turned into butterflies.

On those nights, how was it possible to believe, without forty eyewitnesses, that those same mouths that were quarreling and swearing like stevedores a few hours earlier had become mouths dripping with courtesy and refinement, singing like nightingales? Yes, like his own daughters, those men seemed likely also to deceive a man at first glance. But several had an interior that was more loathsome and deplorable than that of his own girls.

When Master Ali Riza had lost hope of finding the one he sought among these many different types of men, he became resigned to anyone at all.

"With this lifestyle, the girls will either fall into a trap set by one of the rakes, or else will lose their reputations... At that time it will become altogether impossible to marry them... Since I admit that my own girls have not become much of a prize... Thus I have no right to be very particular or selective... I must give up seeking great advantages in them, I can't pause and deliberate and inquire of each one whether he can earn enough to support a household..."

One evening Master Ali Riza spoke with a commission agent who was said to be thinking of marrying Leila. This man, named Master Tahsin, was forty years old. He had been married twice before, and was fortunate in neither marriage. What sacrifices he had made to please his wives. But these ungrateful women had not left anything undone to him and they had escaped after destroying his reputation.

Master Tahsin earned a lot of money through commission work. Some of his enterprises were so successful that they put him among the town's richest men.

Master Ali Riza didn't believe these stories. Who knew what lay behind these fairy tales of goodness, sacrifice and wealth. But there was no cause to believe he wasn't accurate, at least in eight percent of what he said.

If this Master Tahsin wasn't some kind of great scoundrel or embezzler and could earn enough money to support his wife, that would make him good enough to be his son-in-law. For that reason, the old man heard his guest out to the end, and appeared to believe everything he said. Only the next morning when Mistress Hayriye was brushing the table, she found a piece of paper that had fallen on the floor. This was a letter, written by a tailor to Master Tahsin, threatening legal action for fraud if he didn't pay this month the money for a two piece suit that had been made a year before.

There was a similar type of suitor for Nejla who appeared and occupied Master Ali Riza for eighteen days.

He was a serious twenty eight year old child with an aristocratic face. He was a clerk in the post office. His monthly salary was meager. But he said he had inherited money from an uncle in Europe[7] and could spend a lot of money.

When the matter grew serious, Shevket made an investigation and soon discovered that the young man's money came not from an uncle who had died in Europe but from a rich sixty year old mistress who lived in Hisar.

---

[7] "Europe" refers possibly to the European part of Istanbul, which for natives of Istanbul is always contrasted with the "Asian" part of Istanbul, a prominent feature of that city being that it straddles two continents.

XXII

From now on, the idea that he would marry off Leila and Nejla was lodged in Master Ali Riza's brain.

He used to blame himself angrily when he saw his girls dancing cheek to cheek[8] with strange men, or laughing and conversing with them mouth to mouth, or walking arm in arm in lonely places.

But now he didn't feel the old bitterness and shame, and he would close his eyes to all the improprieties, hoping that his daughters would perhaps each hunt down a good husband in this way.

From time to time, new faces would appear in Nejla and Leila's vicinity. Some of these were educated men of distinguished dress.

Every time, Master Ali Riza would be seized by great expectations, and he would put up with their offering his daughters their arms on beautiful evenings, and bringing them back in an automobile late at night from Üsküdar.

But these men were vague shadows who would disappear after nosing around his children for a time, like smoke, seen from afar by a wretch who has met with a disaster at sea and who welcomes it with glad cries of hope, only to see it dissolve into pieces, never to be seen again…

When Master Ali Riza had first gone into society with the seriousness of a great civil servant entering into the directorship of a regional school, the world had suddenly come to a standstill. When he was there, women no longer dared to be too flighty, men to show too much vehemence. But now everyone was familiar. No one thought it necessary to show him respect. Where before they would address him as "your excellence" and themselves as "your servants", now they didn't hesitate to tell indecent stories in front of him. There were even times they teased the old man and hurt his feelings by saying, "May I have this dance with you, your

---

[8] Literally, dancing "against the ear".

excellence?"

And what did Master Ali Riza see, when he sought his son-in-law, sneaking around with his body more withered and his clothes more worn out every day?

Apparently they were having the highest degree of diversion, making a tumult like the day of judgement.

While they were dancing in one room until they collapsed the unsound parts of the floor, in another they had set up a gaming room, and bearded and mustachioed men would perch on arm chairs and flap their wings, crowing like cocks, or would imitate donkeys walking on all fours on the floor and kicking out their hind legs, braying amidst peals of laughter and hand clapping. But it didn't take Master Ali Riza long to decipher all types of intrigues and dramas among the people who in appearance didn't want anything but to go crazy and enjoy themselves in this way at top speed. Either secretly or with a bold openness, they would caress each other, deceive each other, get jealous, try to be corrupted... One evening he saw a woman suddenly faint, another he saw two drunks, with the excuse that they were getting a little air, go out into the garden and break one another's heads.

Sometimes Master Ali Riza escaped the kitchen where his wife was working among piles of dirty dishes and glasses, and went to an upstairs room.

It was here where his youngest daughter Aisha, when she had dropped from exhaustion, would curl up on a cushion stuffed with grass and go to sleep.

On tiptoes, Master Ali Riza would approach his daughter's head and squat down on his heels, and would look at length on his small meager body curled up in sleep, the thin neck, the colorless face, and think: "Ah, at least let me save this one!"

One evening when he was looking at her, he couldn't restrain himself and started to cry, waking the child with the tears dripping from his eyes.

84

XXIII

Another evening Mistress Hayriye came into Master Ali Riza's room holding the coffee tray. "Shevket brought fresh coffee from Istanbul..."

After she left the cup by Master Ali Riza's side, she began to examine the room. "The bed sheet has turned into an oil slicker from grime, Master Ali Riza... Give it to me tomorrow and I'll wash it... And you're coughing again... Tomorrow let me make a tincture and I'll put it on your back... You're not shivering with a quilt? Let me give you my big cloak and you can put it on top..."

This evening Mistress Hayriye's face was as sweet as any angel's. To cook fresh coffee for her husband by hand, to notice the bed sheet had become a slicker from grime, then when she worried that he had coughed to propose to make a tincture for his back and add the winter cloak to the quilt... what extraordinary kindnesses and courtesies were these! But the ungrateful Master Ali Riza, instead of thanking her for these honors of an olden time that could not even be remembered, twisted his face into a grimace and looked his wife up and down and side to side, like an animal who doesn't trust the hand that caresses him.

The woman, after finishing her inspection of the room and deciding the measures that seemed necessary for her husband's happiness and repose, sat by his side and said: "Master Ali Riza, I want to have a little heart to heart talk with you. What will become of us? The Winter is upon us... There's not a penny of firewood or coal in the house... The children have nothing to wear... They have begun to shiver more than ever... What shall we do?"

Furthermore, Master Ali Riza had understood as soon as he saw his wife holding the coffee cup where her talk would lead. He didn't answer but sat, deep in thought, until Mistress Hayriye continued, after waiting a little while: "Did you say something, Master Ali Riza?"

The old man shook his shoulders slowly and heavily and opened his hands: "There's nothing to say, because…"

The woman became slightly cross: "How is there 'nothing to say'?... Aren't you the man of the house?"

Master Ali Riza said, with the poisonous smile that from now on would never leave his lips: "I'm accustomed to difficult times, but it's everyone except me who spent money when there were three or four piastres to spend… Is there a man you're thinking of to get you out of trouble?"

It seemed inevitable that the woman would be enraged by these words, would say serious bitter things and get up and leave. Truth be told, that was just what Master Ali Riza wanted, because if Mistress Hayriye got angry she would be satisfied with screaming and yelling alone, and would depart without asking for whatever impossible thing her mind had proposed. But she didn't get angry, whatever he said, but answered with nothing but a slight reproof: "Master Ali Riza, you didn't used to be this way."

The old man agreed: "You are absolutely correct. I used to be a different type of man. Now my morals are corrupted. I spend money on gambling and women that I bought."

Mistress Hayriye swallowed a few times and bit her lips. But this evening it seemed absolutely impossible to get her to quarrel because she still controlled herself. She said, with the same sweet voice: "Master Ali Riza, be fair. To whom should I tell my troubles if not to you? Whatever you may say, the others are a bunch of children. This house needs both of us. We should talk together, just ourselves."

The old man understood that it wasn't possible to save himself from this danger he foresaw, whatever he did, and so he said, looking as if he had accepted everything from the beginning: "Very well, so be it, Mistress Hayriye, what do you want me to do?"

The thing that Mistress Hayriye wanted wasn't something that was so great. In the last months, Shevket had gotten a little into debt. Now he was thoroughly depressed, constricted from this side and that. Her

86

husband could be of a little help to this self sacrificing child, who for years had taken the house on his neck, in his hour of trouble.

The result of what Master Ali Riza had been worried to learn a moment ago, was that he said with great haste: "This is all very well, Mistress, but you're not saying something that really matters to me. Where am I going to get this necessary money?"

Mistress Hayriye bent her head down with a fearful and shy expression: "I don't know if I should say this but I've thought of a way. Let's borrow three or four hundred lira from the Credit Union[9]... Shevket says he'll pay it back in at most six months."

"Then you've decided to speak with Shevket about this?"

His wife said, as if she was bewildered: "No, not at all, only I can see that our son is very worried and worn out. Ah, Master Ali Riza, you don't know what a heart he has!"

The old man interrupted her with a nervous expression: "Very well, very well... Spare your words... But my understanding is that the Credit Union doesn't give money without security."

"You can mortgage the house, Master Ali Riza."

"!!!??"

"Shevket will pay the debt back by God within six months, or at most a year."

"!!!??"

"Don't you trust your son? Don't you know that Shevket is an honest boy?"

"!!!??"

---

[9] Emniyet Sandik, literally, The Coffer of Security, an institution that lent money on security.

"Give me your answer... Why are you staring at me like that?"

Master Ali Riza smiled as he lowered his eyes: "The world has changed. I understood to a degree that with the world our children had also changed. But what has happened to you, how much you changed, that I didn't understand at all."

Mistress Hayriye tried to laugh: "The things you're saying are ridiculous, Master Ali Riza. Why should I have changed? I'm exactly the same as I used to be."

Master Ali Riza interrupted with a harsh and insulting gesture: "Please... Where is my old serious angel wife, where are you?... You aren't even her lost toenail. Why should I hide what I think? You have become a disgusting creature, Mistress, a disgusting creature... One thing we have is this broken down dilapidated house... And if we lose it, what will we do? Go to die to the neighbors? How dare you propose this to me?"

Mistress Hayriye angrily let fly from her side: "I understand, Master Ali Riza, there is an old proverb that says, 'His father gave a garden to his son, the son withheld a bunch of grapes from his father.' Now the world is topsy-turvy. The son supports his father and the family on his back like a bunch of grapes, while his father refuses to mortgage a house of his for the son. Look, they tell him he's a fortunate father. And why was it necessary to insult a woman like me, tired of her life? Isn't the house yours? If you tell me openly, 'no', the matter's finished, over."

Mistress Hayriye left the room weeping loudly. Master Ali Riza shouted after her: "Go, don't understand that you're wrong, I was only applying to your sense of fairness, to your intelligence. If we lose the house, what will become of us, I said. I am content that you get what you want... I know that you'll never give up anything once you seize it in your claws... You'll take it and break it off somehow, sooner or later... Since it's this way why should I wear myself out and you too in vain?"

Master Ali Riza knew from experience that the next day the whole family would grasp him inside a ring of fire, and he seemed to see as vividly and be as wearied from now on as if he was actually experiencing them, the torments and attacks they would make, the intrigues they would weave until he was forced to cry "uncle".

They were carried along in a wave. What good was resistance? What he had rejected today, when mid Winter came, when the children began to cry from poverty, hunger, and cold, how could he not give in?

The matter of the mortgage was settled within a few days.

From the Credit Union they received up to four hundred lira. But this money, as Master Ali Riza had expected, brought the family temporary relief of at most three or four months.

After Shevket had paid the most urgent debts, the remainder of the money was showered like water on the children. Going to the market after a few tumultuous arguments, they bought heaps and heaps of spangled sequined silk skirts, fake diamonds, boxes and boxes of paint for eyes, faces, cheeks, lips, nails, hair and teeth, openworked stockings, and boots that were like playthings that would strike something and fall apart in the first rainfall. For the reception room, there were a few oil painted pillows, marble statuettes, dolls, nine or ten new Charleston or Tango records.

Two dinner parties were given for their friends, one in Çamlıca, one at home; but Master Ali Riza went down to the Üsküdar market and bought two baskets of provisions and five or six donkey loads of firewood.

The money they had got from the Credit Union was completely used up on the eleventh evening. They didn't have even one lira left from this money. An autumn downpour raged from noon all the way until midnight, and the roof began to leak in a few places.

Under the eaves, the rain fell into tinkling saucepans, jam jars and the laundry basin set out in the upstairs hallway and rooms, and the voice of a continually crying child was heard. This crying child was Aisha. The big ones had clawed to themselves the money, and they hadn't bought the silk dress and pair of patent leather shoes she had wanted for a long time.

Master Ali Riza, at times hearing the jazz band in the sauce pans, at others Aisha's sobs and laments, said to himself: "See we two are ruined! What did I say, I didn't remember that the roof was totally unsound. What could we have done with four hundred lira, melted away in ten days, which should have been money to repair the roof?"

XXIV

That year the Winter was very severe. The streets were covered in snow for days. There were times when wolves came down outside the house in Bağlarbaşı.

The original reason for the mortgage that had been discussed in Autumn was supposedly to affront this Winter.

But the money that was obtained, gone on totally useless luxury, wasn't even spent on flannel underwear for the children.

Thank God for Mistress Hayriye's womanly thriftiness… Whatever rag left from an overcoat or quilted cloak the poor woman pulled out of the bottom of her chest or cupboard corners, no matter how threadbare it was, she would stuff it under cushions and bedsteads. The children would rush toward these rags almost as if they were God sent booty.

For Aisha, whose puny body could in no way face the cold, Mistress Hayriye sewed a cloak from old bed clothes, covering the cotton in diamond shaped layers.[10]

Nejla made a pilgrim cloak out of a table cloth that had turned into a

---

[10] The sense here is a little difficult for me; RNG uses the image of the pastry "baklava" to describe the arrangement of the cotton. My best guest is that it was quilted in "baklava" or diamond shapes to furnish layers that would provide warmth by trapping the air.

90

moth eaten sieve. She embroidered flowers on the edges out of different colored wool.

With these strange clothes, the house turned into a street theater company about to do a production of "The Pink Girl."[11]

Every day, according to the changes in the weather, this wretched old house, like the body of an invalid, burst out in new symptoms of illness.

When it rained, or when the snow began to melt, it would start dripping; when the wind blew, the planks would start, playing whistling flutes in holes in the house's four walls and the sides of the windows.

But the children had accustomed themselves well to the poverty. They didn't appear very sad because of this tragic penury, they even sometimes were hardy enough to make fun of the state of the house and their own clothes. As Master Ali Riza said continuously, they had become wretched creatures without feelings or dignity, like gypsies.

One day the girls, in these strange clothes, joined hands and tried to dance to the rhythm of the rain drops falling in the sauce pans.

When Mistress Hayriye saw Master Ali Riza laughing as he came down a ladder holding a saw, she shouted bitterly: "Long live a father like you. How can you, such a righteous and moral person, not laugh when your children have attained such a degree of happiness!" These words so greatly affected the old man that he collapsed on the tread of the ladder as if he had come down onto his feet and let the saw in his hands fall onto the floor.

*

**

This saw had become Master Ali Riza's greatest helper in this merciless and endless dead of Winter. On the coldest days, as soon as he was

---

[11] *Penbe Kız*, the most famous Turkish operetta.

wrapped up, he would go out and get firewood by cutting down the trees in the garden. What could he do? A man has authority over his property. When the Summer came, those trees would no longer shade the garden. Although for years his hands had toiled to cultivate those trees and they were like almost like his wards, yet nevertheless they weren't the same as the others.

Sickness wasn't absent from the house during the Winter's long continuation. One by one, the children took to bed and would get up. Once even he, Master Ali Riza himself, caught influenza and lay in bed for a week. During this period, no one came to his side; only his wife once in a while brought soup.

"By God's will you will be well today... For Goodness' sake, don't catch cold! It's nothing, it will pass... I'm sick enough to take to my bed, but they don't leave me alone..."

Perhaps Mistress Hayriye spoke like this to excuse herself for not having taken more pains over her husband, or perhaps this was really the way she felt.

His children's neglect hurt Master Ali Riza a lot. In his opinion, in such times a man needed to hear the voices of his family around him, needed to see a living human face. That meant that even if his illness had been more serious, they wouldn't have asked about him, sought him out, and, although he had been so great a man in the house, he would have died alone like someone who falls ill while in exile or in some corner of a hotel.

One evening Shevket came by himself, late at night, and sat on the edge of his bed with a tired and guilty expression. His hand wandered slowly across his father's face to tell his temperature. The only thing he said, taking a deep breath, was, "Father, I haven't visited you."

The young man made neither frivolous excuses or an apology. He was afraid of looking like a shameless liar if he had said something to disguise his guilt, and looked straight in front of himself with a serious

92

expression.

The father and son talked together for five or ten minutes. Once in a while, Shevket coughed very deeply, and would squeeze his temples with his fingertips as if he had a powerful headache.

Master Ali Riza asked, "Are you ill, my son?"

After a slight pause, Shevket said, "No, papa."

Master Ali Riza shook his head with a smile that showed his disbelief: "All right, but just a second ago when your hand touched my forehead, your palm was burning more than me."

"That's just what it seemed like to you, papa…"

"Maybe, my child…"

"I'm just rather tired… with your permission, I'm going to go to bed, papa…"

"Very well, my child… Try to get some rest…"

The father and son parted without meeting each other's eyes, as if they were afraid of telling one another the things that were passing through their brains.

Master Ali Riza blew out the candle by his bedside, and began to think, looking into the darkness: "My son is obviously sick… But I pretended not to know this. But I should have told him to spend about four or five days sleeping in a hot bed in a hot room. But there is no way the wretched child can rest up for several days, or even one day… Early tomorrow morning he knows he'll go out into the street, he'll go one way or another, sick as a dog, until evening, then go to someone's house at midnight. The wretch is more to be pitied than me… At least they leave me in peace in my corner, no one comes to me in my sickness and demands bread… I should even be thankful."

Neither the Winter, nor hunger, nor sickness could impede the party schedule of the house one whit.

The powerful snowstorms stopped the steamboats and trains, but not the evening entertainments in Master Ali Riza's house.

When the evening of the party came, they would pull out as much firewood as had been collected in the house, and whatever there was to eat or drink, they would throw on old cloaks, rough great coats full of holes, pilgrim cloaks made of tablecloths, would dress up in front of the mirror in skirts with plunging necklines, softening their hands, swollen from cold, by rubbing them with lukewarm Vaseline, repairing their head cold reddened eyes and puffy noses with all sorts of paint and creams, chewing gum and gargling with cologne to purify their mouths which stunk from continually eating sausage and pastrami.

They finally came up against the day of bankruptcy, awaited for such a long time. Every day, creditors were screaming at the door, summons came from the civil court.

Shevket would dash out into the black streets of morning so as not to meet the creditors, not returning before midnight. From now on, the feuding and partisanship in the family was over, everyone thought of saving his own soul. There was such brazenness that sometimes they would even be heard complaining that someone or other was knocking at the door.

Ferhunde especially was totally out of control. When she was a little annoyed, if she crossed paths with someone, she would become a mad dog, throwing herself from place to place, "How did I become mixed up with these beggars? They're both consuming my husband's money and hurting my head. If you weren't in my way, we'd be like two little roses," she would scream.

94

Then, while Master Ali Riza would stuff up his ears and escape into the street, Mistress Hayriye cried and screamed and ran from one to the other trying to make peace.

In every one of these quarrels, the family seemed about to collapse and fall in pieces, sometimes Ferhunde would gather up her belongings, sometimes Leila rose and rushed out into the street, saying, "If I can't find any place to go, I'll go into service, or be a waitress in a restaurant."

But perhaps because of Mistress Hayriye's agitation and Aisha's tearful entreaties, or else perhaps it was really the acts of rudeness and malice that were sufficient to quiet their nerves, every time the quarrel would subside and they would make peace with tears and kisses.

Mistress Hayriye, who was always slightly ill in the old comfortable days, had acquired an unexpected resistance. All the house work and the fatigue of bearing up had fallen onto her head, and although her puny body seemed as if it would collapse at any moment, she took on every misfortune with unexpected endurance.

Every day now she would go back and forth to and from the Üsküdar market carrying a bundle. It was understood that she was selling part of the household possessions, and she would come back with a few piastres either for a bit of food or to throw in the mouth of the most vocal of the creditors.

*

**

Master Ali Riza used to get an occasional letter of a few lines from Fikret. These said that, even if the girl wasn't happy, she had been lucky, and they consoled the old man to a degree.

Three or four months before, Fikret had done something silly in one of these letters. "I'm hearing some very bad news about our family, I'm forced to put my hand over my face in front of my husband. Hasn't the time come to put an end to these improprieties?"

Fikret wasn't wrong. What is more, it was also possible that she had been forced to write this letter by her husband. Nevertheless, this reprimand offended Master Ali Riza greatly, and he had said, in the reply he wrote to his daughter: "Everyone is responsible for his own actions. What bond is there between us that you should be affected by things that happen and are finished here? You please me with occasional letters. You see this so clearly, you must know all about it."

Afterwards, Master Ali Riza was sorry for the letter he had written in a moment of anger! But what good was that, what's done is done. From that day to this, Fikret didn't seek out or ask about her father, nor did Master Ali Riza take it into his head to write to her.

In one of the days when the household's financial troubles had reached a peak, Mistress Hayriye approached her husband with a hangdog manner: "Master Ali Riza... We're besieged by creditors... Now Shevket isn't here... The children are hungry... Write a letter to Fikret... Tell her our condition... Isn't she our daughter, let her help us... In the future, if we get out of trouble, we'll pay back our debts... If she doesn't agree, it's not a great loss... In any event, we have a pensioner as a son-in-law..."

Mistress Hayriye was hopeful that her husband, even if he was a little annoyed at first, in the end would say, "Very well." But Master Ali Riza suddenly caught fire, and began to scream walking back and forth with an expression that looked as if he would tear his wife to pieces: "I don't want to hear you saying their name one more time... I'll strangle you... One of our children has managed to escape, now you want to reel her back in? You want to make Fikret open her hand to her husband like a beggar, to shame her, don't you? Don't let me hear you mention her name one more time, I'll strangle you..."

The old man screamed these words with such a savage anger that Mistress Hayriye was afraid and never mentioned her daughter any more.

96

XXV

In the first week of February, Shevket hadn't come home for two evenings running. Ferhunde had been cross at her husband for a week: "He has done this only to annoy me. I'll show him. If he hasn't come back by tomorrow, I swear to God I'll take my stuff and go," she said with irritation.

Mistress Hayriye had another thought. Her son must have gone to stay with one of his friends to escape the creditors. Nejla and Leila from time to time were worried, and said, "I wonder what happened to our brother, I hope he didn't meet with an accident?" But thanks be to God they were preoccupied with more important affairs, giving parties and getting their evening clothes ready, so this worry didn't last very long.

As for Master Ali Riza, like a not very bright student memorizing a lesson, he would sit for hours, his lips opening and closing, without pronouncing a single word. Only, when there was a noise in the garden, or when the door opened, he would shout at the top of his lungs, "Someone has come, run and see who it is!"

On the morning of the second evening, a civil servant came to the door. He gave the news that Shevket was in the prison because of an investigation.

A horrified commotion broke out in the house. Ferhunde fainted, the girls began to weep and cry. Mistress Hayriye, stupefied, could only manage to say, "By God it's not possible, not possible," but at this moment she was forced to leave her own troubles and deal with the ones who had fainted or who were tearing their hair.

Master Ali Riza alone seemed from his expression to have escaped from a great worry. The old man was screaming with an emotion as if he had received pleasant news: "Thanks very much for my son's good health, Shevket is alive!" he was rejoicing. He hadn't given one chance in a thousand that Shevket was alive.

Who knew how or why his nerves had been worn away from age, but a constant fear preyed upon him. "Maybe Shevket will kill himself... My son is a man of the highest degree of honor, he can't hold out against these scandals," he would say, interpreting his son's every word and expression as meaning that he was determined to die.

One evening he rushed out of his room, thinking that the slamming of a door was a gunshot, another evening he shouted when he thought a piece of underwear forgotten on one of the tree branches was a hanging man.

Yes, in his mind, the boy was a child who possessed a great deal of personal dignity. He would absolutely commit suicide if he knew he couldn't struggle any more and couldn't escape from this mud. A few times, he wanted to broach this fear to Shevket and advise him to be strong and patient for a little while longer.

But there was also a danger in this course of action. Perhaps the strangeness that he perceived in Shevket was only his own fancy. He would be like a serious invalid who loses every hope. Probably the young man in this hopeless situation would cling to life more powerfully than ever.

Then if he talked to him about death, he would be the one to force him to think about the final medicine for his troubles.

Master Ali Riza was almost happy, and, taking up his stick, he left the house.

*

**

When the old man arrived at the prison, it was almost evening. At the gate they wanted to turn him away, saying, "It's too late... Come back tomorrow morning." Master Ali Riza began to pester them, no longer being the type of man to be afraid of begging and being insulted. If he had kept it up a little longer, perhaps they would have thrown him out forcibly. But by the grace of God an old acquaintance, an ex head secretary in one of the retinues of his governorships, came out.

98

Recognizing him at once, he approached, and after kissing his hand respectfully, he asked him what he wanted.

The old man said, "They have my son inside… They don't want to let me go to him, saying, 'it's too late,' if you could perhaps help me a little…"

The ex head secretary took a step back, and peered at Master Ali Riza through eyes half opened in astonishment. He couldn't comprehend this dignified, virtuous man whom he had known so well discussing a son thrown into prison for who knew what type of crime.

In any case, this person surely was one of the important employees of the prison, because on his say-so they brought Master Ali Riza to Shevket at once. The old man found his son sleeping with loud snores on a bare wooden bedstead. Although it wasn't the time or the place, an old memory came to life in his mind.

The boy used to like sleeping too late in the morning. When it came time to go to school, Master Ali Riza would tiptoe into his room, and would make a loud sound, either by clapping his hands or by throwing a book on the floor. One he had even played a whistle that was lying on the head of the bed and caused the child to leap bolt upright.

For Shevket to open his sleepy eyes wide and cry out, "Papa, you frightened me to death," was a diversion that he never tired of. From that time to this, so many years, so many events had happened. Between this prisoner and that child, there was nothing similar except the slight bend of the knees and the passing of their right hands over a handful of long hair as they put them underneath their temples. Nevertheless, Master Ali Riza found himself back in those mornings and, what was stranger, he perceived nothing bitter or hopeless in this.

The old man touched his son's head: "Shevket, wake up a little. I've come, my son."

The young man shook himself slightly and opened his eyes, sitting up straight. He too, like his father, showed no sign of emotion.

99

With his two hands joined together, he covered his mouth as he yawned and said: "I was waiting for you, father. When it was almost evening, I lost hope. I couldn't help falling asleep. A bad accident happened to me two days ago. I went and entered into the place I have been."

Shevket, leaning his head against the wall, smiled absently at his father standing opposite him. Motioning to a place beside himself, he said, "Sit down, papa."

Tiredness and tension passed over the young man's face. His cheeks undulated with the light pink color typical of people who have recently escaped the anxieties of a serious illness.

After Master Ali Riza had managed to sit down, supporting him with his cane, he asked, "What happened to you, my son?"

"In any event, you guessed it would happen sooner or later... What could I do, it was written in the stars[12]..."

"This happened because of your debts?"

Shevket hesitated for a moment and seemed to collect himself where he sat. He forgot himself again. He took his father's hand in his own. His eyes fixed on a few points of light that struck the ceiling over the window, he began to speak almost inaudibly: "Unfortunately, my position is a little worse than you imagine... I spent a somewhat important sum of money belonging to the bank... The inspectors came before I could restore it... With this pleasing way of life, I knew I couldn't restore it in five years... You see, once a man loses his head... The result was a filthy business..."

It seemed that Shevket had decided to tell his father the whole sequence of events. But for some reason he suddenly got nervous. When Master Ali Riza perceived that his fingers, still clutching his hand, were pulling back, he said, "Don't have regrets, Shevket, every type of thing can

---

[12] Literally, "written on my forehead"

happen to human beings."

They changed the subject.

Shevket asked about his mother and sisters. In particular, he discussed Aisha at length. Then he began to explain jumbled up things that years ago at times he seemed to have decided to tell his father but had never had the courage.

"You trusted in me most of all among your children, but you received the greatest injury from me, my poor father. How much I wanted to help you in your old age! Unfortunately it didn't happen. However it happened, once I lost my footing, I never recovered. Why would a man like me get married? The absolutely surprising side of the business was that although I saw quite clearly how we were rolling toward a precipice, nevertheless I couldn't do anything to stop it, like a man, held down by the weight of sleep, who understands everything but although he wants to shake it off and get up energetically, he can't even lift a finger... I was just like that... You must believe me, father... Although I seemed not to notice anything, I saw all the dirt... How I was particularly ashamed to come face to face with you. How I cursed myself, you don't know..."

Master Ali Riza stroked his son's hand. "I knew, Shevket," he said, "Never for a moment did I suspect your morals."

Because the time had grown late, Master Ali Riza didn't stay with his son, but as he left he looked around and took note of the things Shevket needed, promising to come the next day. Night had fallen. It was the hour when the day makes even the happiest of men grow somewhat sad. He had left a piece of his own flesh and his own heart in the prison, that grave of human hope and honor. The old man, coming among all this, should have experienced a maddening despair. Yet he, in that moment, not only didn't suffer greatly, but was even a little happy.

When they parted, Shevket yawned slightly, and when he was alone, again seemed to stretch out and go to sleep on the wooden bedstead.

Master Ali Riza was smiling with compassion, like a parent who has left the head of the bed where his child is sunk into sleep after a great tiredness, or after completing a difficult exam.

"What can I do," he was thinking, "at least here he sleeps in peace, the pain of the old weariness is leaving him... There's no one grabbing him by the throat, shouting 'money' like at home, and no one pestering him, when he's not even capable of standing upright, saying 'Bow before us, let's go to a party, to a dance!' "

XXVI

After a short trial, Shevket was sentenced to spend a little more than a year in jail. And so one more of the leaves was lost.

Sometimes Mistress Hayriye looked at her husband very earnestly, saying, "Don't despair, a year isn't a long time, just enough to open and shut your eyes."

Master Ali Riza would agree, nodding his head heavily, but inside he was of a totally different opinion. A little more than a year did seem like just enough time to open and shut the eyes. Only there was this fact too, that, after honor and reputation were lost, they would never come back.

After his son got out of prison, it would really not be easy for him to recover. What would he amount to with this black spot on his reputation, what would he be able to ask for and from whom?

The end result would be that Shevket would be crippled for life, like a man who has lost a leg or an arm. Although the old man knew this well, he wasn't completely despairing. He would console himself by saying, "What can we do, it was an accident... It's enough that my child is healthy, that's what's necessary."

After dry cleaning with gas and ironing one of his old suits and resoling a pair of shoes, he hid them in a cupboard.

This was his best suit of clothes, reserved for the days when he went to see Shevket. He thought the prison employees for some reason or other took special notice of his son, and would treat him differently from the other prisoners. There was no sense lowering his son's status if he came to the prison looking disreputable.

When Shevket went to prison, the six residents of the house had only Master Ali Riza's monthly pension, composed of a little more than thirty three lira, to live on. He begged his daughters, come what may, however they could manage it, to find a husband. But the worst thing about the men who hovered like moths around his daughters in the parties and promenades was that when the talk turned to marriage they would either mince around the subject or else slip away, never to be seen again. They didn't talk about it that much to Master Ali Riza, but presumably the life the girls had led was also a cause that in the end they never came to parlay. From time to time, the old man talked about this with his wife, muttering vague complaints like: "What's the matter with our children? In these times, what girl doesn't go dancing, go out in society?"

At this period, fate was more favorable to Leila. This was a forty-five year old manufacturer who got to know her when she shopped in his establishment. It was said that he was an excellent man at a time of ease and quasi retirement.

As was the custom, Master Ali Riza made perfunctory inquiries at one or two neighboring shops and said, "Very well." Everyone in the household appeared to be glad at this business. But on the evening of the engagement, Leila felt ill.

The young girl began to cry with agitation, saying: "What a pity! Why should I take a father as a husband? Because of your poverty, I'm throwing myself willingly into a grave... Perhaps I would have found someone I wanted if only I had waited a little longer!" And she and Nejla too were wailing and tearing their hair out.

It was true that this marriage was going to save Master Ali Riza from a very precarious situation. Nevertheless, the old man couldn't help agreeing his daughter was right.

For months, for years, he had been angry at his daughters. During this period, he didn't have the heart to look them even once in the face. But this evening he studied them as they wailed chest to chest, and he found his children of an astonishing beauty. What an idiocy it was to be angry with them. In the end, the children were like fingers. They couldn't do anything but flow straight to where the wave of events dragged them.[13] Yes, like Shevket this poor wretch also had to be forgiven.

Master Ali Riza said with unexpected tenderness: "Very well, my child, there's no reason to cry. Since you're unwilling, we too must be unwilling, it's done, finished. Let's see what happens if we wait longer."

Master Ali Riza knew from the very first day that all this evil had come from his daughter-in-law Ferhunde. If it weren't for her, his family wouldn't have come to this, his children wouldn't have been so spoiled. Moreover, she had also been the cause of Shevket's being a thief, of his going to prison. In spite of this, after his son's sentence, the old man had tried to see her in a more favorable light. Sometime he would say to his wife: "Darling... You should treat Ferhunde twice as well, after all she's our daughter-in-law, we owe it to our son... Now she doesn't have anyone but us... She's in a terrible state... Everything has happened to her... After all, our son loves this woman... Now that poor fellow has his hands tied, it rests on us..."

On this point, Mistress Hayriye was in total agreement with her husband...

But the fact remained that however much the husband and wife took the high road, Ferhunde took the low one and quarrels arose out of absolutely nothing at all.

Although in the old days the young woman had shown a certain consideration for Master Ali Riza, now she became altogether brazen with him. She would join with her mother-in-law in insulting him, or else

---

[13] Compare the famous "five fingers" simile in the beginning of Giovanni Verga's *I Malavoglia*.

104

make fun of him with a complete lack of manners.

Sometimes the old man would say to Mistress Hayriye, as if he had quite lost his patience: "For goodness' sake, Hayriye... I want to see you endure this... I don't understand her purpose very clearly, but this woman wants to raise a fuss... Whenever she opens her mouth and says something, she puts all the guilt on us."

Ferhunde had begun to go out with great frequency and return very late in the evening. There were even several evenings that she didn't come home at all, with the excuse that she was visiting a relative in Boğaz.

Finally, again after a few evenings passed with her relative in Boğaz, they received a letter from her: "For years I have been patient. But I can no longer endure the poverty. I'm forced to never ever return to your house. Tell Shevket, see that he excuses me. He would be humane if he easily undid the knot around my foot and let me save myself."

As much as Leila and Nejla had formerly been Ferhunde's friends, now they were her enemies. "Clearly no good will come to our brother from that woman... That was what we knew but we held our tongues... It worked out well... Let her go to hell!" Mistress Hayriye was also of that opinion.

As for Master Ali Riza, he had one more insight. The fact that Ferhunde had left the house meant they were rid of a burden and a problem. But he wondered to what degree Shevket would be troubled? It was true that his son loved this woman. Wasn't that unfortunate love clearly the fundamental cause of this disaster?

The second thing that made the old man think was the question of giving the news of this event to Shevket. No one could perform this delicate duty except for him. First, he absolutely preferred to be by his child's side in this moment. Then, he as a father would certainly do the operation with greater compassion and carefulness than anyone else. It was also even necessary to do it quickly, lest Shevket have the opportunity to learn the story from another.

105

That week, Master Ali Riza found his son sick and in bad humor. This made him hesitate at first. But then he decided that it couldn't come a moment too soon. Especially because Shevket might say, "You had no right to hide such an important thing from me. If you had told me the news when it was fresh, perhaps I would have thought of something," and be angry with him.

After a little small talk of this and that, the old man brought the conversation around to Ferhunde: "God be my witness, Shevket, your mother and I did our best so that your wife wouldn't feel your absence. We treated her better than your sisters. But she wasn't contented at all. She continually complained about us, our house, our poverty... She even went farther, and would say, 'If I were only free I could look after my own head.' "

Master Ali Riza was studying his son's face as if he wanted to understand what impression these last words had created. The young man said with a serious and nervous expression, "In that case, what's she waiting for? The door is open... There's no one restraining her... If she only did this, it would free both me and us from a big problem..."

Master Ali Riza was confused. His heart began to shake with joy and excitement. Did his son really feel this way? If not, was he aware of something from somewhere and was he sounding him out? However it was also possible he was employing these words because these complaints against his wife touched his amour-propre.

Suddenly the old man didn't have the courage to be glad, and said, "My dear Shevket, speak openly with me. Are these speeches true?"

The young man smiled slightly and nodded his head: "Unfortunately, they are true, papa. For me it would be the greatest happiness to sever my connection with this woman."

From that point, Master Ali Riza couldn't speak, his face white as lime, his throat choked up, as he took Ferhunde's letter with shaking hands from his vest pocket and held it out to his son.

106

Because of the darkness in the room, Shevket took the letter over to the window to read it. Despite the fact the old man was caught up by a great excitement, he couldn't take his eyes off his son's face. This was the crucial moment. Now he would learn how much Shevket loved this woman.

The young man read the letter calmly and carefully. He seemed to pause in a few places. Then he turned to his father. Although his face was sallow, he was smiling: "I knew that sooner or later it would turn out this way. But I didn't dare to hope that we would escape so quickly. It's over for all of us, papa."

Shevket and Master Ali Riza sought one another's arms and kissed on their two cheeks. The old man couldn't keep himself from starting to cry: "Is it true, Shevket? You aren't just saying this to console me?"

The young man swore an oath, laughing with joy. "What are you saying, papa? I have escaped from my biggest prison… If they took me out of here at this hour and let me go home with you, I wouldn't be so happy."

But seeing that his father was still not convinced, he continued explaining: "It wasn't that I didn't love this woman at first. But when every day I saw more and more of her seamy side, her strange side, I began to grow cold and loathe her. My eyes wouldn't certainly have welcomed seeing a person that I loved in that type of crisis, that type of disorder!… Loving like every thing is a privilege reserved for people who have a certain amount of tranquility, time and money, father… The result was, that the time came when I began to not even be able to endure that woman taking a breath beside me. You'll say, 'If that was the case, why did I stick it out for years? Why did you allow us and yourself to get into this condition?' It's difficult to explain this to others but you'll probably understand.

I'm not the type of man who can easily throw and shake off something once I've taken up a responsibility… Whatever my hope was, I was compelled to stick it out to the end. This is the way you brought us up. If anyone could say of me, 'He's a captain abandoning ship,' this would be impossible to do. So go back home with a tranquil heart, father. Getting rid of Ferhunde is an unexpected pleasure for me... Relax, don't castigate yourself, saying 'We didn't perform a duty we undertook, we were the cause of the collapse of a family and the swallowing up of a person... In any case, how can such families really be called families? For both you and me to try to be a man resulted in nothing but injury. Come on, let's try to be animals!..."

XXVII

Ferhunde's leaving caused a regime change in the family. Once Leila and Nejla lost their leader, they were no longer in a position of power. For once the rule and the sultanate again passed into Master Ali Riza's hands.

Shevket's arrest obviously had put a stop to the evening parties, the family's habitual guests had scattered. Some thought it dishonorable to be seen with the disgraced family of a convict, others, although they didn't think that, left only because of the sadness and lack of gaiety in the house. The few who remained one by one stopped frequenting the house because of Master Ali Riza's constant disagreeable remarks. In a few months, there was no one knocking on the doors of the house in Bağlarbaşı. From now on, Master Ali Riza didn't consent to his daughters walking about every day from street to street, speaking to one person or another, and if they tarried a little late somewhere the day of judgement would break out. You can imagine how Leila and Nejla reacted to these restrictions! However, a series of events that resulted in Nejla's marriage made them forget the world for a time of about four months.

That Summer Leila had three chances of marriage coming at once, one after another. The best of these was a young doctor named Master Nizam. The attraction for Leila was his face, for Mistress Hayriye his profession and the fact that he was the son of a distinguished family, and for Master Ali Riza his seriousness. The house was happy from head to toe. But a few days before the end of April, Master Nizam let Master Ali Riza know with a few lines that the business wouldn't happen and he went at once to Smyrna. They didn't understand the reason at all. At first they thought Leila's enemies had spread some new calumny about her. But a little after, a new narrative transpired, that is, that Master Nizam's father didn't want to accept as daughter-in-law the sister of a thief, and had said he would disown his son if he didn't give up this girl...

Leila's second suitor was a property manager... He too wasn't a bad man. As to his face, he was even better looking than the doctor. Despite this, without thinking, Leila sacrificed him to the third suitor.

This was a forty-year old Syrian house guest of a family of scribes in Çamlıca.

One day, Leila had seen him in the Üsküdar steamboat and liked him, and at once had decided to marry him.

For some young girls, to catch an Egyptian or Syrian seems a bird of paradise giving them every unimaginable happiness.

The young girl was almost mad with joy when she thought that a rich Arab wanted her. That meant, she had got a great prize that wasn't allotted to one person in a thousand.

Leila had seen that this man's face was half cleft in two. There was no information about how this had happened. But with the power of imagination, she imagined herself as the wife of one of the Hindu rajahs in the cinema whose foreheads sparkle with gems as big as walnuts, and with incalculable expectations she was making extravagant promises to her mother, her father, and her sisters.

From now on their poverty was over. The whole family would live like princes with the assistance of this Syrian son-in-law.

The young girl's crazy hope first infected her sisters, then her mother, and finally Master Ali Riza, who had been reduced to hoping for help from a flying bird. The family made every day a holiday.

Master Abdülvehhap seemed to be as humane as he was rich. He never criticized Master Ali Riza's poverty. "What do I want with money or a name... I'm happy with Mistress Leila just as she is... By God I'll drown her in gold and diamonds," he would say.

Because Master Ali Riza's house was now in such a state that it couldn't be properly called a house, the simple engagement ceremony was held in a pavilion where the son-in-law was staying. Master Abdülvehhap took this occasion to present Leila with a beautiful dress and a pendant. The fiancés would remain in Istanbul until the end of September, then, again after a simple marriage ceremony, would depart for Syria.

Master Abdülvehhap began to frequent the house in Bağlarbaşı regularly.

He took every opportunity to say, "Don't worry, be at ease... I'm not looking to find fault... Don't go to any trouble for my sake... By God, even a glass of coffee isn't necessary," by no means wanting them to get into difficulties to honor him. Whatever Mistress Hayriye did, she knew she couldn't show respect to such a distinguished person; rather, whatever happened, the family was acquiring respect.

The furniture that had been set out in the reception room as being appropriate for the old evening parties – since a few of the pieces had been sold – was now put into a guest room as being more appropriate to

111

a bourgeois home. As for Master Son-in-Law, he was taken straight there, and honored with coffee, tea, and, when the ice cream seller passed in the street, ice cream.[14]

Because Master Abdülvehhap seemed a conservative man, and continually talked about religion and morals, Mistress Hayriye too from now on had changed her strategy.

When the girls were a little too flighty, when they talked and laughed too much, she would signal them with her eyebrows. She was terribly afraid it would offend Master Abdülvehhap's old world ears.

She even tried to get Nejla to wear her veil when she was in the presence of her brother-in-law.

Leila thought her mother's strategy was correct, and she was now playing the role of a girl of the old times who didn't care too much for elegance and diversion. Why did she need to hurry? She would take a husband who was twenty years older than she in the palm of her hand and make him do whatever she wanted. There was a long life in front of her to be happy however she thought best.

Master Abdülvehhap promised, when the time came, to find husbands, as rich and as worthy as himself, for his sisters-in-law.

For this reason, Nejla and Aisha neither put him on the ground nor in the sky, but fluttered around him like moths saying "brother-in-law".

As for Master Ali Riza, he was naturally grateful to an angel come down from heaven in the form of a tall Arab with camel ears, to save his children from a real disaster. But nevertheless in his heart he didn't feel as much trust for this man as seemed necessary, from time to time he was suspicious of certain words and expressions. But in these hard times he needed so desperately to believe and cling to something, that he attributed the suspicions that awoke in his mind to the pettiness of his

---

[14] In the text, dondurma, a special kind of very stiff Turkish ice cream.

heart. "I have been a very bad and unjust man... In reality I'm guilty of the sin I attribute to the poor fellow," he would say. Then he was so thirsty for words like "morals, virtue, righteousness," that whatever mouth they came from, they would be welcome to his ears.

Master Abdülvehhap often took Leila for a walk and she would come back in the evening holding a small or large package.

A black velvet coat especially made the young girl crazy with joy. After Leila, who had had trouble controlling herself and remaining serious in Master Abdülvehhap's presence, came back, she wrapped herself around her mother, her father, her sisters, and then inside her room danced for minutes. When she pressed one of her cheeks to the collar of the velvet coat, her eyes closed, as she turned round and round waltzing the waltz she had learned from the gramophone, it made Master Ali Riza's eyes water involuntarily. The children really were as big as these fingers. When it came to their nature, they were neither bad nor good. If a breeze began to blow from one side or another, they were carried along in front of the breeze like leaves, blown straight along whether they wanted to go to one side or another. How a little hope and money had changed his daughter whom he had thought would no longer go on the path.

After Leila had finished dancing, she paused in front of Nejla, and threw her hands around her sister's shoulders with the free and easy assurance of a protector. "You don't want me to give you this bride's fur coat of mine, do you Nejla?" she said.

Master Ali Riza saw Nejla suddenly shake herself free and look at her sister for a moment with an expression full of bitterness and anger. Suddenly his heart ached.

This meant that Nejla was jealous of her big sister. As the old man left the room smiling to himself, he thought: "O God, what an empty dream it is to expect happiness from one's children! This is inconceivable, given the nature of our hearts. If it was in our power to make everyone of our children happy, the happiness of one would obviously be lopsided in reference to the happiness of another... At that point we would at once forget their happiness… We would cry as we heard the voice of the one and only child who was unhappy… Yes, to expect happiness from a child, from a descendant, is an empty dream."

*

**

The time when Leila was to go to Syria was approaching. Master Abdülvehhap seemed very pleased with his fiancée. But one day from nothing a quarrel broke out between them. When Leila crossed paths with some old acquaintances in the steamboat and the market, she pretended not to see them and didn't respond when she heard them coming toward her. But one evening when she was strolling with her fiancé on the Çamlıca road, she ran into a group of eighteen of them, men and women. She couldn't escape because there was no room. Inevitably, she stopped and chatted, even was forced to introduce Master Abdülvehhap.

Annoyed by this, her fiancé got angry, and began to say things to hurt Leila's self respect. The young girl answered rather sharply and that evening they parted in anger. Master Abdülvehhap didn't drop by the house for a week afterwards. A powerful fear seized the whole family, starting with Mistress Hayriye.

At last a piece of news reached Master Ali Riza from the fiancé.

Leila had talked with several unsuitable individuals in the street and, what was more, had defended them to her fiancé. A reputable man couldn't endure this state of affairs. Consequently, it had become impossible for him to take such a girl. But because he liked Master Ali Riza a lot, if he gave him the little sister, Mistress Nejla, he would accept her with pleasure!

For a whole week, Master Ali Riza and Mistress Hayriye had eaten Leila alive, saying, "You did something bad, you offended your fiancé." But as

114

soon as this piece of news came from Master Abdülvehhap, they suddenly understood the reality of the matter.

Master Ali Riza's intermittent fear had proved justified.

This fellow, whom they had never even examined as to who and what he was, was not a shoe that was sound in any way. Perhaps because he had tired of Leila after two months of strolling at her side, or perhaps because he found Nejla, younger by two years, more fresh and beautiful than her sister, he had taken into his head to leave one and take the other.

In the final sequence of events, they had accused Leila unnecessarily. Their little daughter was not at fault. This anger was only a pretext invented to get rid of Leila and take Nejla. And it was a pretext savagely primitive!

A revolution of cries of horror broke out in the house. For Master Ali Riza the best course of action consisted of returning this man's engagement ring along with a few presents – giving them to the man who brought the news. As a matter of fact, the old man would have had no hesitation in doing this. But at that time something happened that was less imaginable than Master Abdülvehhap's proposal.

Nejla placed herself opposite Master Ali Riza, with a greater maturity than could be expected from her years, and said, without thinking it necessary to be embarrassed or ashamed: "What are you doing, father... Are you crazy? Would you stand in the way of my chance of a match? Since Master Abdülvehhap wants me... If you give me to him instead of my sister, it's over, done."

Master Ali Riza's tongue was frozen by this degree of boldness, which he never could have crammed into his mind; Leila fainted. Only Mistress Hayriye, despite great emotion, didn't lose her composure. "Nejla's opinion isn't totally wrong... Let's reflect a little, Master Ali Riza."

That evening there was a long and tumultuous conclave in the house. Master Ali Riza didn't want to consent to this marriage at all. Moreover, in the first place, what could you expect from a man who committed this kind of immorality? To such a tramp, not only wouldn't he entrust his daughter, he wouldn't even entrust his house cat.

In his opinion, the street beggars with their cups[15] were a thousand times better than this shameless and unscrupulous man. Secondly, he thought it very shameful for Nejla to be married to the man who had seen fit to do this awful thing to her sister.

Mistress Hayriye agreed with all her husband's opinions. This Master Abdülvehhap was truly an immoral man. No one would certainly even entrust his house cat to anyone like this. But what use was that, it wasn't the moment for these arguments. The children had become more despicable and insignificant than kittens. The debt to the Credit Union remained the same. The house would be sold soon, and the children in the middle of the street. They had not a single solitary expectation from anywhere. The earth was iron, the sky copper.[16] Although all of her husband's reasoning was good, saying "no" wasn't correct. He should be grateful that his decision was really not so important... The last word belonged to Nejla.

The last word? Nejla listened to this argument with the peace that is proper to people who have taken a decision, and smiled involuntarily. Hadn't she given this last word in the very moment when they got the news?... Now she was listening to her father and mother quarrelling unnecessarily, without moving a hair, as if it were fairy tales, thinking of her happiness, occasionally looking out into the darkness from the window. What had been born when the day was born? That the bird of fortune sitting on her sister's head would have taken flight and alit on her own head, if she had seen it yesterday at the same hour in a dream, she wouldn't have believed in her fortune... Now for her there was only one thing worthy of thinking about; that was tying up tightly the bird of

---

[15] Keşkül, a beggar's cup shaped like a boat and made of either metal or wood.

[16] Compare *Deuteronomy* 28:23 (the curses of Moses), presumably also found in the Koran, although I couldn't find it.

116

fortune, so as not to give it liberty to play the same trick on her it had played on her big sister.

All day long, Leila had resented this action of her sister. At last she couldn't hold out, she began to snipe at her while she was speaking with her father. There is no more natural thing than this for a person who has suddenly lost every hope. The most fundamental right of someone whose soul is on fire is to cry. As a matter of fact, the most fundamental duty that fell to Nejla was to recognize the rights of this girl who had lost all her hope, come what may not to seem pleased in what she did and said this evening. Clearly this too for her wasn't a very difficult sacrifice. For a victor to be good and merciful is the easiest and most common of gestures. But somehow Nejla didn't think this magnanimity necessary. She didn't even hold back from lightly mocking her sister. That time, Leila totally lost her mind and a red day of judgement broke out in the house.

The young girl attacked Nejla with the coarse, rough words of a fishwife: "Strumpet... Immoral strumpet... You wanted my fiancé from the beginning..." and her sister, without thinking it necessary to be afraid or draw back, replied: "I have done well, you were greedy and received your reward."

Mistress Hayriye tried to restrain Leila from coming to blows, while Aisha had barely managed to get Nejla out of the room.

As for Master Ali Riza, he had squatted down at the bottom of the wall, with his head in his hands, and was crying with gasping sobs, not so much for what had happened as for his children's descent into vulgarity and baseness.

When Nejla escaped Aisha's arms, again and again she returned, spitting out all her heart's hatred and bile with unspeakable words: "Were you as crazy as I, who had to wear a coat that cost two paras[17]? Without being

---

[17] A para is one fortieth of a kurush (piastre), which is one hundredth of a lira (pound).

ashamed, you acted like the angel girl to me... Look how God turns people like you topsy-turvy... When you got your Winter fur coat, you gave your old coat to me, didn't you? Now I'll give it to you gratis as alms for my marriage."

XXVIII

15 days later, Nejla and Master Abdülvehhap set out for Syria. Thus the third leaf broke off from the bough and was lost.

Between Nejla and Leila there was something much greater than sisterhood. The difference in their ages was minimal. Their faces and their characters were similar. They slept in one bed, grew up together, and they laughed and cried together.

In Master Ali Riza's opinion, they were a couple who couldn't conceivably live apart from one another, the most perfect model of something called ties of blood and family. However, they had parted as two blood enemies who would never again meet face to face.

From this point on, the family was diminished. There were no other children at home besides Leila and Aisha. At once Master Ali Riza sold the house in Bağlarbaşı. All their debts were paid. With the remaining money, he bought a house on Dolap Street.

118

It was a broken down dark place with two big rooms. Compared to this, their old house that they had all with one accord dubbed "Gehenna" was like their summerhouse in the Garden of Eden. But with the money they had, it wasn't possible to buy anything better. Mistress Hayriye hated it at first glance: "If we'd waited, maybe we could have found something a little more palatable…" But Master Ali Riza, who had become a totally different person from the old Master Ali Riza, laughed with bitter derision: "Should we have waited? Was there some booty to be scrambled for? So you could have squandered the five or ten lira I had like last year's money and left me in the street?" he had said. The children entered the house in tears as if they were entering a grave. And Master Ali Riza's impression was totally the same. But nevertheless, when he took his first step across the threshold, he involuntarily touched the key he was holding to his lip, praying, "May God not show our poverty…"

*

**

Leila hadn't yet recovered from the recent events. On the second day after they had moved into the house, crying "My head, my head," she took to her bed. She lay down for forty five days without moving her tongue or mouth. Thank God, the illness wasn't anything serious. A retired doctor who resided in the neighborhood said, "Nerves… You should make her eat and drink well… Don't trouble her… It's nothing." As the doctor said, a good month later Leila got up from bed. But as a totally different Leila, it was as if during her illness one evening someone had removed her from her bed and put someone else in her place. She was very thin. She moved with difficulty like a child who has just begun to walk, and once or twice she put her hands over her face, darkening her eyes. Although her countenance had changed, she was still beautiful.

Because the illness had brought a sort of mildness to her countenance, Master Ali Riza found her even more beautiful than before.

Like her face, Leila's character had also changed. From now on she wasn't cross whether there was reason or no, and bent her neck completely to her destiny. Master Ali Riza noticed that his daughter's eyes were constantly covered with a slight vapor. The old man imagined that when she spoke and smiled to her interlocutors, she was crying deep inside herself, but the tears were so fine that they transpired like fumes without falling as droplets. This was perhaps from an old fear that enfeebled her nerves. But in any case it awoke inside Leila a strange compassion.

Then the old man's feelings of love began to reawaken. All the grudges that he had against his daughter were lost and erased.

A little after Leila got back on her feet, she began to go out. The doctor was saying that they should make her take strolls and enjoy herself, even if possible give her a change of air. The change of air was an impossibility.

The old man was very pessimistic, so much so that he had food prepared that was suitable for one who was gravely ill. But nevertheless Leila was able to get out once in a while to take a stroll.

The first time, Mistress Hayriye, after wrapping up her daughter in a cocoon, helped her up into a cheap hackney[18] and took her to take the air at the seashore. That day, as Master Ali Riza passed the time in a small room by the street door, he felt his heart fill with life.

Mistress Hayriye, embarrassed as if by a sin, had left a bundle beside Leila. This was the well known velvet coat left by Nejla for her big sister, as "alms for my marriage."

Those words that Nejla had screamed on the evening of the quarrel with rapacious insolence, at this moment really were ringing in everyone's ears. But here there was no one at all with the courage to say that he remembered this, because then it would be necessary to throw this costly

---

[18] The text reads paraşol, which is given as paraçol in Redhouse, "a light one-horse carriage without springs."

coat away.

Mistress Hayriye took courage from Leila's lack of peevishness, her silent sitting lost in thought, and she said hoarsely: "Come on, daughter… Put this on and let's go."

The old woman waited, standing holding the coat, turning her face sideways so as not to meet her husband's gaze.

When Master Ali Riza saw his daughter again bring her hand to her face, as if darkening her eyes, and rise bit by bit from her place, there was a lump in his throat.

*

**

From now on, Leila wore the velvet coat every day, and would take herself and stroll from street to street.

At first, Master Ali Riza didn't think anything about these walks. What could you do, the child was in pain. He knew from experience that nothing dissipated anxiety about something like aimless haphazard walking in the city and the countryside. And even if that weren't so, it wasn't as if the house in Dolap Street was a real residence. Especially in the short days of Winter, two hours after noon it was so dark that they couldn't sit in the rooms without a light. But as time passed, thoughts and fears began to awake in Master Ali Riza.

For a young girl to wander so much wasn't a good thing. Especially since sometimes she would stay out very late. And then she had maintained relations with the old party people.

Leila's old vivacity and health had returned. But because Master Ali Riza still looked at her as an invalid, his tongue was completely incapable of saying anything to hurt her feelings.

A little later, this vague fear took the shape of a danger that he could grasp in his hand.

122

Things sounded in the old man's ear that somewhat disturbed his stomach. But what a pity it was that this time Leila's great freedom acquired a strength of custom, and with time had taken on the nature and power of a right. If in spite of this, Master Ali Riza had wanted at times to warn Leila, he wouldn't have made himself heard, and if the matter was investigated more thoroughly, he himself had not thought very much about it. This struggle that had continued for years had tired the old man out and worn him down.

In the end, he had quite lost his trust in the effects of advice and talking. Whatever a man said, things would come out the way they came out. The result was that Leila continued to go wherever and do whatever she pleased.

XXIX

The news coming from Nejla grew worse gradually. On the road, the young girl had learned that the luxury and riches she expected from the Arab was nothing besides her own fancy.

Master Abdülvehhap wasn't the rich millionaire he claimed to be in Istanbul; he was a man who lived hand to mouth from a few confused bits of work that were as hard to explain as they were to understand.

In Beirut, Nejla had moved into a small house that was a chicken coop compared to the palace of her imagination.

Instead of manservants arrayed down marble staircases, she was greeted by a father-in-law in a galabia, two co-wives, and a troop of children.

The third co-wife had died nine months before. Since Nejla had come to replace this woman, it was natural that from now she would take on the duty of being the mother to the two children that were hers.

The young woman, like Nasreddin Hodja's tree[19], understood that whatever good luck she saw or would see consisted in one or two bits of things she had taken when she left Istanbul, and began to show a little temper. But when she saw that, at the first signs of a quarrel, the galabia clad father-in-law came at her, singing out with a booming trumpet voice, she became ill at ease and afraid and no longer had the courage to open her mouth.

This life, among the two co-wives and more than a half dozen children, was unendurable. But at first Nejla was ashamed to write this to her family, being especially afraid of giving joy to Leila. But after a few months had passed, she couldn't hold out, she got over her embarrassment and shame and began to let out her complaints bit by bit. Then step by step they increased.

In her last letter, she said "Papa, I can't endure it. If I can find a way, I'll kick everything over and escape to Istanbul. I would be happy with your dry bread crust.

I can't stop thinking about my mother and my brother and sisters.[20] My big sister Leila never leaves my mind.

Once my sister regretted not marrying this man. Now if she saw what I endure here she would really thank me for her escape."

When Leila read this letter, she forgot all her grudges: "Dear papa, let's rescue Nejla," she said, as she threw her arms around Master Ali Riza's feet.

Mistress Hayriye was also more or less of this opinion. But the old man

---

[19] Nasreddin Hodja is the subject of many folk tales. He was a famous Islamic judge born in 1208, and the reference to the "tree" probably refers to the famous story when a passer by notices the judge up in a tree cutting a branch and warns him that the branch he is cutting is the one he's sitting on. (from http://www.allaboutturkey.com/nasreddin.htm)

[20] Literally, My mother and my siblings are smoke in my eyes.

turned a deaf ear to these entreaties, and this was the way he answered in the letter he wrote to Nejla: "The things that you relate have affected me a lot. But what use is it, when I am in no position at all to help you? Now that we are poorer than ever, what would you do if you came here? There, if your house and your husband aren't of good quality, at least he is a man of good reputation and he is sufficient not to make you in need of help. You should grit your teeth for the inevitable and get used to the people around you, my daughter."

With this letter, Master Ali Riza was explaining openly that his door was closed to Nejla from now on. But the young woman would become so depressed that she wasn't ashamed of something very disagreeable, and pled for help in letters she sent one after another, saying: "Rescue me; if not, I'll kill myself, you're threatening my life!"

This "I'll kill myself" of Nejla was really an empty threat. But it could have been otherwise. What can you expect from spoiled children with confused minds that change from one moment to the next?

The old man would say to himself peevishly, like someone who is answering a sound that keeps on annoying his ear, "We have understood, our children are falling leaves... But out of five children, can't one at least escape?"

XXX

One day, a retired major, one of Master Ali Riza's coffee house friends, drew him into a corner, in one of the Üsküdar cafés: "Master Ali Riza, my brother, there is a matter of great importance that I have to talk to you about... I hesitated for a long time... But because I loved you and recognized that you were a man of an impeccable reputation..."

The major stopped when he saw the old man had grown pale and begun to tremble, but after a short pause, he said, "You're probably hurt."

Master Ali Riza at once got control of himself. There was no sense in

125

scaring off his friend by doing something irrational.

If this preamble was any indication, the thing he was about to hear would certainly touch upon his family life. But come what may he absolutely had to learn the truth.

The old man said, with a voice that was as calm as possible, "Don't worry, I can endure anything."

"But do you promise not to be hurt?"

"If you put your hand in fire, you can't help but be burnt... But I'll do my best."

"But this isn't really something to make too much of... The thing that I wanted to say is this... You shouldn't allow your oldest daughter to wander about so much, maybe it would be better if she didn't go out at all for a while."

"What is it? What happened?"

"Nothing... Just that a young girl at that age, it's not right to allow her so much liberty."

"You changed what you were going to say... You know something... Tell me the truth, what happened."

The major said after a second hesitation, "Very well, I'll tell you what I know... Last week, I saw your daughter getting into an automobile with a very well dressed young man. You can't guess how worried I was... Three days ago our children said other, further, things. Perhaps I'm exaggerating, but..."

The major was waiting for Master Ali Riza to ask him again to relate what the others things were. But from that point on, he was not capable of looking at this man's face or asking for anything new.

Saying only, "Has this too befallen me?" he stood up and, as if night had fallen suddenly in the street and he didn't see where he was stepping, he

126

began to walk with a heavy tread, feeling the paving stones with his stick.

He kept asking, in a voice that the approaching nightfall could hear, "Has this too befallen me? I was hungry, disgraced, I endured every type of insult. I put up with everything. But I didn't endure my family's losing its reputation… There is absolutely nothing to be done…"

Suddenly something occurred to him as he came upon his house: "The major knew other further things… I left the fellow's words in his mouth. Whatever it was I should learn everything. I need much more knowledge to be able to do anything."

At once, Master Ali Riza turned back. He went down the hill as fast as possible, fearing that his friend had left. This fear was well founded, because when he came panting to the café, the major was on the point of getting up. From then on, Master Ali Riza overcame his embarrassment and shame, and implored his friend to tell him what he knew.

He received this full explanation: Leila for almost two months had been the mistress of a lawyer who had a wife and children. Two days a week, they met on the Üsküdar wharf and went by automobile to a love nest in Haydarpasha.

If there was a lie in these words, the sin belonged to those who had told him. But this was a story that had almost reached the mouths of his family.

When Master Ali Riza again reached his house, night had fallen. As soon as Mistress Hayriye saw him, she said, "Leila hasn't come home yet, I wonder where she is?"

The old man made a motion as if he couldn't think of Leila because of his weariness and collapsed on a sofa beside the door. He didn't want to tell Mistress Hayriye about this narrative before he interrogated his daughter again, since he didn't trust his wife.

It was very possible that Mistress Hayriye, although she had heard

127

something from someone else, had concealed it from him. And even if not, being very afraid of her husband's anger, she would come to Leila's defense and would explain things to her by winks and movements of her eyes.

While Master Ali Riza sat on the sofa and prepared the questions he would ask Leila, Mistress Hayriye and Aisha were in the kitchen preparing supper.

After ten minutes had passed, an automobile horn sounded at the street corner and a little afterwards a rapid footstep approached the house. The street door opened; Leila came in. moving as if she was afraid of making noise and walked straight towards the light coming from the kitchen. When she saw her father rise from the sofa where he sat in the darkness, she gave a light scream.

"Is it you, papa? You frightened me to death..."

Aisha, when she heard her big sister's voice, came out from the kitchen holding a light. Behind her was Mistress Hayriye with her sleeves rolled up.

The old woman said, "Where were you at this hour, Leila? I was crazy from worry."

"Nowhere... I was with a friend... Wait, let me catch my breath and I'll tell you..."

Leila hadn't yet thought of a tidy and well planned lie. To gain time, she asked Aisha for water and drank it.

Master Ali Riza stood beside the staircase, his face couldn't be seen in the darkness. He asked with a calm, dignified voice: "Did you come in an automobile?"

Leila said after a barely perceptible pause, "Yes, a guest of my friend brought me."

Master Ali Riza, in spite of his desire not to give anything away at once

128

to his daughter, couldn't control himself: "Are they that kind of home owners?... They bring guests home in an automobile... Can we know who this friend was?"

"You wouldn't know them..." Leila continued, turning to her mother, "My friend was going to the dressmaker in Haydarpasha. She insisted on bringing me... It wouldn't have been natural to turn down a free automobile ride. But we stayed a little late."

At this word, "Haydarpasha," Master Ali Riza lost all his caution. "Is this the first time you went with your friend to Haydarpasha?"

The young girl said with surprise, "Yes."

"I don't think so... What street in Haydarpasha is this dressmaker on?"

Leila again turned to her father and tried to make out his face in the darkness, to see his eyes. The old man seemed to know something. Although a little earlier, when she had come through the door, he seemed to be holding something back, this time she didn't attach a whole lot of importance to this, but said with the peevish voice that was proper to the times when she wanted to frighten her father: "But really, father... You're asking questions like it was the last judgement!"

This impertinence enraged Master Ali Riza. The old man walked over to his daughter and started to scream with a fearsome anger all the things that he knew.

Mistress Hayriye threw herself between them, saying, "Master Ali Riza, get a hold of yourself... It's a lie, a slander." If Leila had done the same thing, even if she hadn't said anything, the old man perhaps would have still hesitated. But she stood with her hands on her hips and wrapped herself in the velvet cloak like Spanish actresses on the stage who turn their bodies wrapped in fringed shawls a little sideways, and said, "What happened happened. If you were a man, you wouldn't have reduced your daughter to this condition!"

The light held by Aisha struck Leila's face, and her painted mouth

129

twisted up with contempt and mockery, her eyes constricted by disgust within black hoops, blazed up giving Master Ali Riza the impression of a corpse.

The old man suddenly grasped his cudgel with a fearsome anger, "Clear out, get out of my house, now!" he screamed.

This time Leila was a little frightened, and drew back to the door.

"Wait then, who do you say is staying? God damn your house!" she answered.

Emotion gave the old man the power of a wild beast. Mistress Hayriye and Aisha wrapped themselves around his arms and legs, but he shook them off like two bundles of cloth and rushed at Leila. This attack was so unexpected, that, if Leila hadn't gathered herself together and escaped, even if she hadn't died at the foot of the door, she would have suffered some grievous wound. But Master Ali Riza, as if his foot was suddenly stuck in the floor, fell face down, and his staff landed two feet away.

XXXI

Master Ali Riza had suffered a light stroke. After that evening, his chin pointed a little to one side. His speech was somewhat indistinct. When he walked, he dragged his left foot slightly. But if you saw him, you wouldn't notice this. The real illness, eating and consuming him, was in his heart.

Most of that first period, because the man didn't have the heart to go out, he passed in the small room. Opposite the window was a wall, half collapsed by fire. Every day the old man stared at the tenuous greenery sprouting from the wall's hollows, at the cats hunting lizards among the stones. One of his occupations was trying to create a new sundial on the principle of the light that moved upward bit by bit, starting at the middle of the wall until it reached its position at noon.

130

After Leila left, the whole family became idle. Mistress Hayriye, who for years had struggled and toiled with a power that came from some unexplainable part of her puny body, suddenly was lost. It seemed like soul wearying drudgery to wash the dishes once in two days, to occasionally put out a plate of foot, or to run a comb through Aisha's hair.

The old woman was like a soldier returning from a long and bloody conflict. Now she felt the ache of the wounds she had received and the endless weariness, everyday she perceived some sickness or infirmity somewhere.

The matter of Leila had affected her, just as much as Master Ali Riza, in her heart's most sensitive place. Because it had been a question of reputation, she didn't fault her husband for the anger he had shown, but at the same time she couldn't help but feel a baseless disgust and anger at him. Although the husband and wife were home all day and all night, sometimes they would go a couple of weeks without exchanging two words.

This state of affairs seemed to Master Ali Riza at times an inexplicable riddle: "We have lost our children one by one... We have been left totally alone by ourselves like when we were first married... Doesn't it seem necessary, contrary to what happened, that after this misfortune we should be forced to feel much closer? Whereas we are almost disgusted by one another... Lord, this human nature is such a strange riddle!"

Master Ali Riza found the mate of this riddle in both his and his wife's relationship to Aisha. After having had six children, only this one little girl remained. In this situation, shouldn't they give Aisha the love they had for all the others, love her six times more? But instead they treated the child like a cat wandering around inside the house, to be pushed and shoved whenever it got under foot. It was obvious that there wasn't much difference between children and a set of china. If they all got broken one by one until just one remained, it became useless and would be thrown into a corner.

Aisha was now fourteen years old, and had begun to be beautiful like her sisters. But whose eye saw her Springtime?

The old happy talkative Aisha had become a fearful child. As if there was an invalid or a corpse in every corner of the house, she didn't dare laugh, talk with a loud voice, or walk fast, but at the first opportunity would run into the garden or to the neighbors.

A few months later, Master Ali Riza became accustomed to this misfortune. He began once in a while to take his stick and go out into the street. Finally he passed in front of his old cafés. His friends tapped on the windowpanes and called out to him. After a few coquetries, he went inside. The way they treated him, compared to the old days, wasn't very different. If you thought clearly, wasn't this right? After he learned that Leila had fallen into a bad way of life, if he had kept the girl at home, they would have been right to say that he was disgraced. But since as soon as he had learned the truth, he had thrown her out and hadn't pronounced her name any more, in this case didn't it seem necessary for them not to make any difference between him and a father whose child has died, and even to pity him a little?

XXXII

Although the other children were occasionally mentioned in the house, Leila's name was never uttered. Only one evening Mistress Hayriye absentmindedly called Aisha "Leila" and then, when she covered her eyes with weariness and lay down to sleep, she explained to Master Ali Riza that she thought about her always.

On the wall there was an old picture taken when Master Ali Riza gathered the children together and brought them outside. The old man had cut with scissors and removed from this picture Leila sitting at the bottom of his feet, so that only the hands embracing her father's knees remained. This was an idiocy that children couldn't understand. One day when Aisha was looking at this picture, she had said, "Look at those

132

hands, papa... Isn't it my big sister Leila embracing your knees and pleading with you?"

On the subject of this opinion, Mistress Hayriye, not clearly understanding that it came from naivety and wasn't a ploy, suddenly began to sob. Master Ali Riza threatened the child with a shaking fist. "Brat... Don't let me hear you pronounce this name once more!" he screamed.

However, from that day forward the spell was broken. Mistress Hayriye began to talk about Leila frequently, without paying attention to her husband's fits of anger. At first she took every pretext to tell stories about her childhood. Then she passed on to news about how she was now, things that had come to her ears from someone or other; they said he wasn't a very bad man for a lawyer who had corrupted a poor girl.

Leila was living very well in a small apartment she had rented in Taksim. He even also wanted to marry her, but what use was that when he couldn't find a way to separate from his wife. Moreover, rather than from immorality, this man had done this to Leila because of love.

Master Ali Riza said, "For the love of God, be quiet, Hayriye... I'll die from shame," but although he closed his ears he was also not displeased with the news. After all, a child is a child.

From her place, Mistress Hayriye was learning how everything was. One evening the old woman informed her husband that Leila had been sick in bed for fifteen days. "The wretched child is a rotten thing... I'm afraid. You haven't gotten over the sickness you had last year."

This word "sickness" awoke a small feeling of mercy and love toward Leila in Master Ali Riza's infirm heart.

The vision of Leila's acting, her impertinent expression as she posed with hands on hips, wrapped in the cloak, her painted mouth twisted sideways and her eyes constricted with contempt inside a black hoop, was suddenly lost and another of a sick and hopeless Leila in bed with a wilted face came to life.

133

Mistress Hayriye took courage from the sadness in her husband's face. "Give your permission.... I want to see my child once," she pled.

Master Ali Riza wasn't angry, but said only: "Is this speech a speech that should be heard coming from the mouth of a respectable woman like you, Hayriye? She's dead, it's not possible to meet her again face to face!"

But at that moment involuntarily two tear drops fell down from his eyes. To show that this weeping was a sort of discomfort caused more by the light, the old man looked directly into the flame. Afterwards he bent his head forward and left the room, dragging his sick foot more than usual. Mistress Hayriye didn't believe in this naïve stratagem.

*

**

In Mistress Hayriye, who was suddenly letting herself go, showing a weariness where it was unnecessary to open her eyes once in a while and look about her in bed, or even to answer questions with the tip of her tongue, in those days after the Leila affair there began to appear certain signs of an unexplained awakening. Once in a while, the old woman would lift up her skirt and go around cleaning the house, making food, visit the neighbors. She also changed her treatment of her husband. While she slunk around Master Ali Riza, she would do him little and unimportant services, she would try to conquer his heart with sweet talk.

This liveliness seemed to his attentive scrutiny the signs of her first defeat, it was so like the state of affairs at the time when the house was agitated as children came on the scene one by one. Master Ali Riza didn't think this change boded very well, and thought to himself: "Wait, let's see... Something's going to appear underneath this," but said at once, "Don't be dissatisfied with God's benefits."

The old man wasn't mistaken in his guess. Without the passage of much time, the secret of this extraordinary service came into the open. One day when Master Ali Riza came through the door holding a cloth bundle of
134

vegetables, he found his daughter Leila facing him.

Leila was in a flutter, crying and saying, "Father, my daddy" as she threw her arms around Master Ali Riza's neck, while Mistress Hayriye and Aisha held his feet and beseeched him.

Master Ali Riza retreated step by step until he had his back against the wall. He covered his eyes. No emotion at all appeared on his countenance. Only lifting his head up into the air as if it was difficult to breathe, he was trying to unbutton his collar with his hand. So this was the reason Mistress Hayriye had spoken so frequently about Leila. They had concocted a plan to bring the girl secretly to see him.

They had tried to soften him with reminiscences pertaining to Leila's early childhood. Then the illness story had been invented. Finally, taking courage from the fact that he no longer showed anger or harshness, they made this raid... The plan wasn't at all bad... Master Ali Riza perhaps wouldn't have accepted it if they had said only, "Leila wants to reconcile with you." But if he suddenly saw the girl's face, perhaps he would be conquered by emotion, without having time to think, he would embrace her... It was clearly not improbable that this raid would kill the father, since he was sick... But what raid could one think of that didn't have an obvious possible danger of three or five percent!

Leila stopped talking, Mistress Hayriye was speaking, when she finished imploring him, Aisha began, and they were all weeping from one throat. Master Ali Riza's hand was still on the button of his collar, and he didn't open his eyes, as if he wanted to be faithful to his oath not to see his daughter any more in this world.

Finally his turn to speak came. The old man said with the peace of those to whom there is no other road to travel, "You're wearying yourselves in vain. I no longer have a daughter named Leila. We must be considered as dead to one another..."

Mistress Hayriye, Leila and Aisha continued to try for more than half an hour, but they received no other words from Master Ali Riza's mouth.

XXXIII

After Leila had gone, a big argument broke out between Master Ali Riza and his wife.

Because Mistress Hayriye understood that she wouldn't move her husband with sweetness, she suddenly raised the flag of rebellion.

"I know you are a man, for thirty years I haven't disobeyed you. What has happened to us is public. Now forgive me, and let me too speak for once. Because of you, every one of our children has been harmed in some way. Aisha and this Leila are the ones that remain. My child cannot live without me. Neither can I live without her, the whole world could call Leila bad if it wanted, for me she would be better than all of them. Either we live with Leila, or..."

Mistress Hayriye didn't finish her sentence, but began to cry.

Master Ali Riza smiled and said, "Don't be upset, Mistress, don't be upset. I like you have taken my decision. I'll leave. Perhaps, God willing, you'll be better off. From now on, sleep more easily, mind your own comfort."

*

**

Master Ali Riza had really taken his decision. Whatever happened, from now on he wouldn't stay in this house. Early the next morning, Mistress Hayriye saw he had prepared his bundle and scolded him like a child: "Please stop this foolishness... You're a crazy old man... Where are you going to go in this state... Here there are still places where you can go and wander about... There's no need for useless scandals."

Master Ali Riza invented a lie to get out of the house without a ruckus and bad words: "I'll stay for a few evenings with my milk brother in Pendik... I'll come back again."

136

His purpose was to go to Fikret. The whole evening he had thought over the words she had said to him in the Haydarpasha station: "If you're very miserable, you can come to me, papa... My husband is a good man, if it comes to that, I'll look after you as best I can."

In this there was a secret hope. Perhaps Fikret would take him in, and thus he would escape living in poverty and infamy. Although he didn't want to be a burden to any of his children, what can you do; God's will can't be planned or stopped.

It was really this hope that drove Master Ali Riza, until after an hour, late at night in Adapazar, with the help of a policeman, he found his son-in-law's house at the end of a dark street.

He found Fikret clearing the table in the dining room, and when she saw him, she said, more from fear and indecision than surprise, "Is it you, papa?... You are well, by God's will?"

Master Ali Riza kissed his daughter's hand with a cold expression; not having the courage to embrace her, he grazed her shoulders with his finger tips, noticing two children looking shyly at him. Then he saw in the door of one of the rooms a tall, white mustached man.

The young woman said, as if ashamed of this shabby old man, covered in dust and dirt and twice as decrepit as usual from road weariness, "My father has come to be our guest."

Guest... What did Master Ali Riza feel about this word, which it seemed necessary to use when he came through the door?... With these two words, didn't Fikret mean to imply to her husband, "Don't worry, or be angry... After one or two days he'll be gone."

The son-in-law approached Master Ali Riza with a cold expression. He gave orders to Fikret: "Your father has been travelling. He's hungry, prepare a meal."

The farther that the old man put his foot into this house, he understood from the air striking his face that his daughter wasn't happy here.

Inside a few years, Fikret was almost broken, she had become a middle aged provincial woman. As she came and went preparing food for her father, constantly scolding the children, she showed all her peevishness.

A little afterwards, while Master Ali Riza tried to eat the plate of potatoes she set before him, they asked about what was happening in Istanbul. When they were alone, he would without doubt tell his daughter everything.

Only, however it might be, in front of his son-in-law, a stranger, suddenly he didn't want to open up any more. He tried to be done with these night long questions and answers with some lordly responses.

But in spite of the fact that they hadn't learned even one in ten of the things that had happened, they began to show signs of nervousness and anger.

The son-in-law said: "As a matter of fact, we have heard some things."

Fikret scolded him with a frown: "Ah papa... Don't be cross but most of the fault is yours... You know how I struggled to say 'Papa, open your eyes! All these men are tramps... It's not seemly to give your beard into their hands.' You didn't listen, you didn't listen..."

Her husband, taking courage from her, began to say more severe words: "Fikret is right... You are a man who saw your day, you discharged great duties... You shouldn't have been so weak... 'This is the way I want it, this is the way it will be,' you should have said. Whoever opened his mouth, hit him below the belt and kick him out... It would be finished, gone... If I had been the home owner, the father, as Fikret said, and I trusted my beard to my children... What could happen but this?"

As a matter of fact, Master Ali Riza was choking from the weariness of the road and he felt a knot of food morsels lodge in his throat. With a bitter smile, he twisted his neck. "What could we do... Destiny... Fate..."

There was the widowed sister of Fikret's husband in the house with two

138

other children. Since there was no other empty room, they made up a guest bed for Master Ali Riza by the side of the door.

They didn't keep Master Ali Riza in Adapazar for more than 15 days. And that with such pestering! He found Fikret such a stranger that he didn't tell her any of the things he wanted. And since it was impossible for his daughter, even if she wanted, to let him live with her, why did he need to tell her anything?

Although his daughter had promised, "If you're in great trouble, come, papa... We'll look after you!.." nevertheless this too was connected to a stipulation. He remembered very well that time when Fikret had said, "Perhaps one house will be peaceful." But that hope of the wretched child had been in vain. Here was another type of Gehenna. Here life was poverty under another form.

Master Ali Riza saw that Fikret wrestled almost every day with her mother-in-law, her sister-in-law, her husband, and her step children. Thank God that his daughter had become a woman with teeth and a tongue.

Master Ali Riza had begun to be aware that some of these quarrels were also on his account. One day Fikret made his ears ring with her yelling, when she said to her mother-in-law, "Don't let me hear you say my father's name once more. I'll pull down your house on your heads!"

So as if it wasn't enough what Fikret had to suffer in this family, there were additional problems coming from him.

The old man told Fikret that evening, as he did every time when she came into the guest room with a pile of quilts for the guest bedding, "It tears my heart apart to see how you tire yourself out for me, Fikret, but this is the last night... If you give permission, I'll leave tomorrow."

When Master Ali Riza said, "If you give permission," he was like a disgraced man escaping from a duty for his own purposes.

After Fikret was done with the bedding, she said, "Why this haste, papa?"

"It's not haste, dear, but I've seen you so…"

After Fikret had thought a little, she said sadly: "Father!"

"What is it, dear?"

The young woman seemed to have decided to tell him something very important.

But after a short hesitation, she gave up, as if she had decided it was unnecessary.

"Then you're travelling tomorrow," she said. "At least go to bed early… May God give you rest."

After she left, the old man thought: "From where do I remember this expression, this phrase?" He soon thought of the answer.

His son Shevket in the past had spoken this way a few times.

Conclusion

After Master Ali Riza came back from Adapazar, he didn't go to his house. He wandered from one place to another like a tramp, spending two days here, three days there. Finally, towards the Winter he got sick; his left arm and left leg became totally immobile. He was checked into the hospital with the help of one of his old acquaintances. But he didn't remain there long. One day Leila and Mistress Hayriye came to the hospital in an automobile. Weeping and weeping, they wrapped their arms around Master Ali Riza.

Leila said, "Papa, we're not leaving you out in the world."

Hayriye started to beg him, "Master Ali Riza, from now on stop being stubborn, do a little of what I say!"

Mistress Hayriye's fear of her husband's stubbornness was a vain fancy. Age and sickness had enfeebled his nerves, had withered his rebellious streak from its roots. He wasn't surprised at how his daughter and wife looked, wearing such fancy clothes, he was happy as a child to see them again, trying to say things to them with a tongue that from now on had grown totally heavy, without repressing the tears in his eyes he was heaving great dry sobs as if he had the hiccups.

Mistress Hayriye had rented out the house in Dolap Street, and together with Aisha had moved into Leila's apartment in Taksim. Because Leila's lawyer could escape from his spiteful old hag of a wife only two nights per week, the poor child was living almost alone with a servant girl in the huge apartment. Leila had a lot of free time. The lawyer, being rich, gave her a few hundred lira per week. What use was that, since, being an inexperienced child, she didn't know how to make use of them. Now praise God her mother had become the perfect housekeeper to sate her, lock stock and barrel.

In this apartment, for Master Ali Riza, they prepared a pretty room facing the sun and the sea. With comfort and abundant food, in the shortest of times, the old man improved markedly. With his stick, he would walk

142

around in the house and tried to give language lessons to Leila's parrot without noticing his own slowness of tongue.

Sometimes the lawyer's friends even organized diversions in his apartment in his honor, and sometimes they would go to help Mistress Hayriye in the kitchen as she prepared hot food and appetizers, sometimes they would rise to distribute drinks with Aisha, who was now a beautiful 15 year old girl, or, when forced by the guests, they would even have made the council chamber merry getting up to dance joyful dance numbers with women.

When he tired of staying at home, they would dress him up in clean proper clothes and take him to get some air in an open carriage...

In those days, Master Ali Riza was as happy as children who get into the festival cradle[21], with festival clothes. Only, if he once in a while in the crowded streets came face to face with some of his old coffee house friends...

---

[21] This possibly has something to do with beşik alayı, the procession of the cradle, in honor of a new born royal prince.

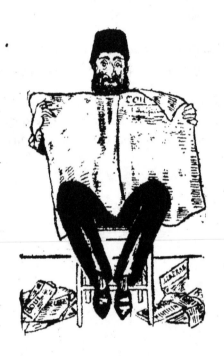

CPSIA information can be obtained
at www.ICGtesting.com
Printed in the USA
LVHW081749130521
687357LV00012B/839

9 781491 073964